Echoes of Her

Brooke Kenny

ALL THINGS
THAT MATTER
PRESS

ISBN: 978-0-9846297-2-5

Library of Congress Control Number: 2010916383

Author photo by: Susan Whitney

Cover Design by All Things That Matter Press

Published in 2011 by All Things That Matter Press

To Ed,
who cherishes and protects the flame
even when I think I want to blow it out.

Acknowledgments

I have been lucky enough to stumble upon many creative souls, including the members of my writer's group, Pamela M. Ehrenberg, Gwen Glazer, Farrar Williams, Elizabeth McBride, Meredith Narcum Tseu and Kirsten Green. I'm certain you don't know how much you helped with this project.

Also, to E. Ethelbert Miller for being kind enough to open up to a crazy woman who accosted him at a Takoma Park coffee shop, asking if he was an editor because she saw him carrying a stack of manila envelopes. Said woman shall remain nameless.

To Elly Williams for agreeing to be my thesis advisor and for the subsequent hours she spent scratching out the "ing"s at the end of every single verb in an early draft of this book. I owe you another cartridge of red ink.

To John Bond and Carol Ann Erskine for helping me understand military life so my characters could ring true.

To Deb and Phil Harris for taking a chance on me.

To the Kennys for taking me seriously and letting me cry over this book at the dinner table.

And finally, to my mom, who teaches me the meaning of determination every day.

The most common ego identifications have to do with possessions, the work you do, social status and recognition, knowledge and education, physical appearance, special abilities, relationships, personal and family history, belief systems, and often political, nationalistic, racial, religious, and other collective identifications. None of these is you.

—Eckhart Tolle

ONE

The truck was audible from four blocks away. It was a moving van, the bargain kind, and it grumbled and hissed along the roads of Gemstone Terrace, finally coming into view as it rounded the corner onto Nacre Court with a series of squeals.

When the neighbors pulled away their sheer drapes, their Venetian blinds and their hand-crocheted lace curtains, they saw the van door open and a greasy, crumpled fast food bag fall out onto Julie Curran's driveway. A thin, muscular arm appeared, lighter than ivory and wrapped in a blue linen shirt rolled up past the elbow. The full view of the young woman followed as she jumped out of the cab, her flip flops smacking on the black pavement. Her face was round with thin black eyebrows, a thin upper lip, and a tiny button nose. She wore no make-up; her bangs minimized the appearance of a large forehead. She was altogether tomboyish but also undeniably cute. They saw her take a moment to look around, her knotted dark ponytail moving as she scanned the street. Her surveillance started where Nacre Court intersected Emerald Drive and ended near the golf course pond. The large cattails around the pond's edge swayed patiently in the wind.

Tulsey was suddenly aware of how steady her nerves were. This was the first time she had broken out of her own mold, but it was a welling sense of general unease rather than a breakthrough that had led her here. The old life was behind her now, yet she couldn't even muster enough concern to be mildly anxious.

Julie appeared from the side door of her house, little Lila in her arms staring at the stranger.

"Welcome, Tulsey," they heard Julie say. "It's nice to have you here." The young woman smiled and shook Julie's hand, then gently took the little one's hand and shook it, too. Julie pointed to the door of the apartment above her detached garage and dug into the pocket of her jeans, producing a key strung on a red shoelace. She held it out like a pendulum before Tulsey clasped it in her hand and put it around her neck. Julie said a few more things, but they all heard different parts, depending on which way the breeze was blowing. Something about the stairs being shaky but structurally sound, then something about extra room in the garage, and eventually a final welcome from Julie before she and the little girl turned and disappeared through the side door.

Tulsey walked to the back of the truck and took hold of the rusty latch. She lifted and freed the breadbox metal door, then watched as it snapped up with a billowing crash that irritated the quiet. She must have pinched her thumb, because she let out a resounding "fuck" and sucked the tip of it. She shook her thumb loosely in the air before she reached for the retractable metal ramp. She strained to get it loose; her backside stuck out and her heels dug into the ground as she yanked, readjusted, yanked again. The ramp rolled out slowly, foot by agonizing foot, and when she finally placed the end of it on the driveway, she sat at the base and wiped her forehead with her shirt. She disappeared behind the truck for a few moments, and when she returned, the top of her hair was wet. She rubbed her hands over her face, then ran a hand down each arm. Water? From an outdoor faucet? Garden hose head. Dirty, rusty garden hose head water smeared all over her face. This woman was to be their new neighbor. Julie Curran was so desperate for help that she took on this woman?

She took two liquor boxes overflowing with old pans, magazines, stuffed animals, a jump rope, fake roses, half-burned candles and a wooden tennis racket and made her way up the unsteady stairs to the door of her new apartment. She tried first to unlock the door with both boxes in hand but then abandoned them on the landing to struggle two-handed with the apparently stubborn lock. Removing tattered boxes two by two, she made a dent in the contents of the truck, then opened up the cab, leaned into the driver's seat and came back with a purse over her shoulder and a cell phone to her ear. She spoke almost incomprehensibly fast to the person on the other end of the line, flipped shut the phone and dug her hand into her purse, pulling out a crumpled pack of cigarettes and a lighter. She cupped her hand over the flame and inhaled, then put the lighter in her pocket and sat on the truck ramp looking around, sucking deep drags that she exhaled into thick streams of bluish white.

When she finished her cigarette, she flicked it through the air and into the grass. It landed only inches from a fat gray squirrel greedily digging the insides out of an acorn. The animal was so startled that it darted to the nearest tree trunk, leaving the half-eaten acorn to roll to a stop, unattended in the grass.

"Sorry." Tulsey watched the squirrel dash up the cracked bark. She walked over and stomped on the still-smoking butt before she leaned down to pick it up.

Ten minutes later, a yellow Geo Storm rolled onto Nacre Court with the rhythms of Eminem beating out of its rolled-down windows. A robust man with a full strawberry blond beard and matching curly head of hair hoisted himself out of the seat, still rapping the lyrics. He wore dirty construction boots with ribbed white socks that reached the base of his thick calves, and the sleeves of his stretched T-shirt hung loose around his wide arms, reaching almost to his elbows. He tucked his keys into the pocket of his khaki cargo shorts and set to helping Tulsey do her heavy lifting. The mattress, the box spring, the cheap brown metal roll-away frame, the poorly hand-painted yellow bedside table, the rolled blue carpet, the dresser, the chintzy gold-framed poster of a tiger, the ironing board, the stereo system. They carried a series of tools into the garage, stopping occasionally for a chat and a smoke. The neighbors couldn't hear what Tulsey and the man said, but they could periodically hear her sharp laugh pierce the heavy summer air.

The day began to fade and one by one, porch lights came on. Golfers took their last shots before they slid their putters into their bags and drove their carts back toward the clubhouse. Lightning bugs flashed. Tulsey and her companion stared into the tree branches, heads flipped back like Pez dispensers, before she finally looked at her friend and said, "Only the vanity is left. Let's finish. I've got to take the truck back."

After all the junk they had collectively seen go up those wooden stairs and into that tiny apartment, the neighbors each leaned closer to their windows and watched with great interest as Tulsey and the man lifted what appeared to be an antique vanity table, adorned from top to bottom with thousands of pieces of mother of pearl and finished with delicate handles and brass-clawed feet. Thousands of dollars? Tens of thousands? Tulsey had purchased it at a church flea market for forty bucks but figured it was worth more like two hundred. They lifted it carefully, first down the ramp. Before they made their way up the stairs with it, they paused for a moment to rest and readjust their grips. The deep, dusky light made the whole of the white table glow as though it were a ghost perched silently before the house. It was spectacularly beautiful, and the residents of Nacre Court all opened their mouths a little in disbelief and mild confusion as they watched this ghost dance up the wavering stairs, turn the corner and disappear through the door.

Moments later, Tulsey broke the spell when she flipped on her porch light and the moths descended on the naked bulb. She and the man quickly went down the stairs, lifted up the ramp and pushed it into the base of the truck, pulled down the back door and twisted shut the latch. Tulsey climbed into the cab, fired up the wheezing engine and rumbled up Nacre Court, the orange glow from her lit cigarette dancing in the dark outside her open window while the man followed close behind in his tiny yellow car.

***

The first night in her new apartment, Tulsey hadn't been able to find where she had packed her bedding, so when she awoke the next day, she had to figure out why she was sleeping in yellow drapes, a beach towel bunched under her head. She swatted at the alarm, then took a long sip from the Big Gulp of Coke, now watery and flat, that sat on her nightstand. She rubbed her eyes and looked around. Her window let in the first sunrays of the day — the day she was to interview for a job as a receptionist at Shaw Marketing.

She showered and put on the black skirt and heels she hadn't worn since her cousin's wedding two years earlier. She took out her dusty cosmetic bag and unscrewed a bottle of liquid foundation, but found it was dried up and so had to settle for face powder. The mascara she brushed over her lashes made her sapphire eyes stand out but caused them to water, and some of the mascara ran down her cheeks. She wiped her face clean and put on sheer pink lip gloss, admiring herself in the mirror for a moment before fastening some of her hair back in a beaded barrette.

Tulsey didn't have a briefcase, so she slung her backpack over her pink cotton blouse and headed out the door to the bus stop on Emerald Drive. Before she left her hometown, she had mapped out her entire route. She would have to catch the number sixty-three bus before transferring to the number five, which would drop her at the corner of Banneker and Franklin, right in the middle of downtown. From there it would be a six-block walk to the office.

Tulsey watched through the tinted bus window as it pulled past Gemstone Terrace with its newly clipped lawns and freshly painted, closed garage doors. No garbage cans sat out, and she did not see a single bicycle left by a child on one of the smooth driveways. All of the streets in the neighborhood were named after gems, and a large gray stone gateway stood watch over the entrance to the neighborhood. Across the street sat a strip mall, which, in addition to a dry cleaners, post office, comfort shoe store and gourmet grocery store, hosted a coffee shop named Navajo Joe's. For all those Navajo on the East Coast?

She stared at the endless streets of nearly identical houses going by, and she realized that Valiant, her new home, was a city in its own right, lumped with other cities much like it in the wings of a thumping metropolis. It looked to have good restaurants and clusters of new and expensive stores inspired by the charm of 19th Century towns. It had a lot more grass for children to play on than the city row houses.

When Tulsey got to Shaw Marketing on the seventh floor of Somerset Tower, Suite 714, the blisters on her feet throbbed. She was half an hour early, and she had to sit in the overly air-conditioned waiting room trying not to pull off her heels so she could rub her aching toes. She traded uncomfortable glances with the receptionist and wondered if the woman knew that she was there to interview for her job. She told the lady that her interview was at 10:30 a.m. with Robin Marks. She asked her to wait until 10:25 to call back to Ms. Marks' office so that she would not look overeager. The receptionist nodded and straightened her headset before answering a call.

At exactly 10:27, Robin Marks blew through the door, blond hair bouncing and expensive perfume billowing around her. She greeted Tulsey quickly and took her past several rows of gray cubicles on the way to her office. There it was, Tulsey thought when Robin swung open the door. A real professional woman's office with a flat-screen computer monitor and a view of the courtyard and fountain down below. She could tell a lot about Robin just from the way she set down her keys on the desk and moved her computer mouse to see if she had gotten any new emails. She had gone to college, she was obviously bright, but most importantly, Tulsey knew Robin was clear about what she wanted and was unapologetic about getting it.

Tulsey sat across the desk and Robin pulled out a crisp blue folder with a gold Shaw Marketing emblem embossed on the cover. Robin opened it with the long, manicured nail of her right index finger. She read over it, her eyes visibly scanning from line to line, before she looked at Tulsey and began a rapid fire of questions — everything from "How do you handle conflict in the work environment?" to "What do you think you can bring to Shaw Marketing?" Sitting in the throne-like black office chair, her crotch sweating in the taupe nylons that she had bought back home at the Thrift 'N Save, Tulsey handled the questions as quickly as they came.

"I'm a tremendously hard worker," Tulsey said. "Always have been. I was raised a farmer's daughter, so I've always had to balance a lot of chores at home with work and my social life. And I love working with all kinds of different people. That's what makes life interesting. I don't judge anyone for being this or that, I just do my best to get along with them and work with them to get the job done."

Robin paused, her eyes looking down at the blue file folder before looking up at Tulsey with her piercing green eyes. "Why would you say you did not feel it necessary to go to college?"

Tulsey's breath quickened. "I thought I was headed for a life of farm work and that I didn't really need a college degree for that. I've been training to do that since I was five years old. But recently I decided that I didn't want that life for myself."

"And what do you want for yourself?"

"To be a professional woman. To better myself intellectually so I can build a life outside of where I grew up."

"Farming's a hard way to make a living?"

Tulsey nodded. "But that doesn't bother me. It's just the idea that I'd be stuck doing it because I was groomed to do it. You know, everyone wants a choice about where they end up."

"I see." Robin scribbled something on Tulsey's résumé. "I must say, we've never gotten a candidate for receptionist who was from out of town. I'm not looking for someone who is going to do this job for a couple of months and then give up when the first disgruntled client gets nasty."

"I'm not a quitter." Tulsey pointed to the résumé. "Aside from all my work on the farm, you can see that I had been working at the same job at the local deli for seven years."

Robin nodded her head ever so slightly. "I think that's all for now, unless you have any questions for me."

"Just one," Tulsey said. "What's your favorite part about working here?" She leaned forward toward Robin. Robin flipped back her hair and stared briefly out the window before she answered.

"I've worked my whole life to be where I am now," she said. How old was she? Tulsey wondered. A few years older than me? Mid-thirties? "And I have earned the respect of so many people around me. I have finally achieved what I set out to, which is not just to make a living, but to make a name for myself."

Tulsey couldn't have described what she thought were her own desires any more accurately. This place would be good for her. It wasn't perfect, but it was a start. She thanked Robin, then left after a handshake and the assurance that she would hear back by the end of the week.

That evening, Tulsey carefully hung up her skirt and shirt and looked around at all the unpacking she had left to finish. The pictures still weren't on the walls, her books were all over the floor in piles, her toiletries were still sitting in a bag on top of her computer monitor. She walked into the kitchen and opened the empty refrigerator and imagined it full of brie cheese, strawberries, and pie. She pulled the canned goods from the box she had stacked under the window and unloaded them into the pantry, only to take them out again when she decided she should wipe down the shelves first.

When she had stacked the cans of beans and peaches and the boxes of Rice-A-Roni and cereal in the pantry, she looked out through the kitchen window across the street. She saw a thin man with curly blond hair and glasses come out of a two-story brick colonial and get into a silver BMW. The ultimate yuppie, nothing short of gorgeous. Incredible. He pulled up Nacre Court, and Tulsey grimaced at the grime caked onto the kitchen window.

She reached under the sink and pulled out a roll of paper towels and a bottle of Windex. It wasn't just the inside that needed work, so Tulsey lifted the screen, sat on the ledge and cleaned the outside, too, her legs dangling short of the kitchen floor. Her mom would have yelled at her if she had seen her doing this, but she had done it all the time at home, usually waiting until her mom had left the house. She could easily wedge herself through even small open windows. It was one advantage of being barely five feet tall. When she finished cleaning, she looked out through the gleaming panes at Nacre Court, the large white house next to the good-looking guy's house, now glowing orange in the evening sunset.

She returned to her bedroom and changed from her cut-offs into khaki shorts, brushed her black hair and pulled it into her standard ponytail. She smeared fruit-flavored Chapstick across her lips and looked at her white skin in the mirror. She swallowed hard. Her stomach rumbled in trepidation. Tonight she would have dinner for the first time with Julie and the kids. In the interview with Julie, much to her own surprise, she had fielded her questions with relative ease. She loved children — took care of her best friend's son all the time. She would be available three afternoons a week and one weekend day. She was not certified in child CPR, but she would be happy to sign up for a class if required. She wanted to move away from her small hometown so she could expand her opportunities. Farming was the only way to make a good living in Lichten, and though it was the family business, it just wasn't for her.

Tulsey pushed away thoughts of accidentally cursing or saying something that would make Julie change her mind. She opened her screen door and headed down the rickety stairs to the Curran's front door. She rapped on the thick wood. Julie appeared from the side of the house.

"Come on in this way." Julie went inside and Tulsey tentatively made her way along the chipped stone path and in through the screen door. Julie was already down at the end of the hallway.

"Hope lasagna's okay," she said over her shoulder.

"Great. Thanks." Tulsey made her way along the plush cranberry carpeting and found Julie in the kitchen at the end of the wood-paneled hallway. She was kneeling down to look into the stove while Matthew and Lila played separately with brightly colored toy cars on the cream tile kitchen floor. Dark green granite covered the countertops; the appliances were all stainless steel. A breakfast nook with large windows faced the back deck. Drooping plants hung from pots attached to the ceiling, and a single white-washed wooden bench offered a place to sit and think. Tulsey was sure it didn't get a lot of use in this household.

"Why don't you take a look around, get familiar with the house. Or better yet, Matthew, why don't you give Miss Tulsey a tour?" Julie said. Matthew leaped up and ran past Tulsey into the hallway.

"Follow me." He drew out the last word as if he were begging to be called on in school. Tulsey walked back down the hall where framed landscapes, family collages and an unattractive picture of a polo match decorated the walls. She found Matthew in the living room, a bright and spacious area, a large bay window framing the golf course green and the pond.

"This is the room we can't come into," Matthew said.

"Why not?" Tulsey asked.

"Because Mom says we have to keep it clean for guests. I can't come in because if I did, Lila would want to come, too, and she always makes a mess."

Everything in the room looked perfect. The magazines were all neatly tucked into a basket beside the couch. No toys lay on the floor, no fingerprints stuck to the windows. Tulsey could see the tracks from where Julie had pulled the vacuum cleaner over the carpeting. A large family portrait hung above the fireplace in a gilded frame. It had to have been taken recently, as Lila looked about the same age as she did now. In her fluffy pink dress, she flashed an enormous smile. Matthew's smile appeared forced and awkward. Julie wore a blue dress, her neck adorned with pearls as she sat next to her husband, Mark, dressed in his Army uniform. Mark's baby face and closely shorn hair made him more adorable than handsome.

"Let's go upstairs." Matthew's thin brown hair bounced as he shot across the hallway and up the stairs. He walked right past Lila's room — which Tulsey could see was painted with pink and yellow elephants — and went into his own room. The walls had blue trim and the bed frame was fashioned after a red and yellow race car.

"I really like your bed." Tulsey crouched and touched one of the painted wheels.

"Me, too. My daddy made it for me."

"That was very nice of him, wasn't it?"

Matthew nodded his head and pointed out his toy chest before losing interest in the tour and running back downstairs. Tulsey stood in Matthew's room for a moment, considering whether it was appropriate to continue to look around. She headed for the guest room, telling herself that Julie was too busy to hold her hand through everything. Julie and Mark's room had a king-sized bed with a floral bedspread that had been neatly pulled up to the headboard and topped with several coordinating decorative pillows. A bay window, panes on either side, looked out over the back yard. From the window, Tulsey saw that the next-door-neighbor's house looked significantly neglected compared to the other two neighbors' homes on Nacre Court. An old wooden fence, partially rotted and listing badly under the weight of ivy vines, separated the Curran's yard from this neighbor's. The house was missing two black shutters; a third had fallen away from the side and hung upside down by one nailed corner. The paint was chipping off the front porch columns and the grass in the yard was long, unruly and scattered with dandelions and buttercups.

She noticed two striking magnolia trees at the end of the court — heavy with pale pink blooms — that stood large and majestic at the very edge of the neighbor's yard. Someone had placed large pieces of rough white quartz at perfect intervals around the base of each of the tree. Tulsey was surprised to see such attention to detail in an otherwise unkempt lawn.

On her way out of the master bedroom, Tulsey looked at the top of the tall dresser and saw a framed copy of Psalm 23. She had several friends who had enlisted after high school, and all of their parents had copies of Psalm 23. They must hand them out at basic training, she thought.

She returned to the kitchen. Julie was spooning small bits of lasagna onto the plastic table of Lila's high chair. Strings of her own hair were hanging loose from her ponytail, and Lila reached up and grabbed at them, leaving a smear of red tomato sauce on Julie's blond locks.

"Dinner's ready." Julie looked up at Tulsey. Under the harsh light of the stainless steel kitchen lamp, Julie's face looked to Tulsey as if it were almost gray. Her high cheek bones protruded sharply from the sides of her face, and her brown eyes were sunken and surrounded by bluish skin. Tulsey hadn't noticed any of this when she arrived the day before. Maybe it was the lighting. Julie had typical good looks – long golden hair, full lips, naturally tan skin, a thin frame and a relatively large chest. She was the type of person who looked as good in sweat pants as in an evening gown and four-inch heels. Tulsey had always wanted to trade her boy-like physique and light skin for a more bathing suit-ready body. About the only thing Tulsey wouldn't have traded with Julie was her eyes. Tulsey's were an unusual dark blue that nearly glowed beneath her black mane.

Julie took a checkered dish rag and wiped off her hair. She sighed and stood. She made her way to the sink to wash her hands.

"Can I help with anything?"

"Thanks, but I think I'm okay. Matthew, take a seat at the table." She turned to her son. "It's dinner time."

The lasagna was a little bit burned but still edible, and Tulsey ate as she watched Matthew struggle to use his spoon.

"So, you said you work for the school system," Tulsey asked.

"I'm a sign language interpreter. I usually work about fifteen hours a week. There hasn't been that much need recently for interpreters."

Tulsey took a long drink from her glass of ice water. "I'm really grateful for this opportunity," she said. "Rent is pretty expensive around here." She looked at Julie's tired eyes. Tulsey wondered if she had children if she would turn them over to someone who responded to an ad placed in the local paper. She, Tulsey, could be anyone. A pedophile. A thief. Anyone at all.

"Since you don't have a car, you'll have to drop me off at work in the mornings if you want to use the minivan during the day," Julie said.

"That's no problem. I realize that me not having a car is something we'll have to work around."

"And no smoking in the house or anywhere around the kids."

"Of course."

Julie pushed the lasagna around on her plate, took a tiny bite and swallowed before speaking again.

"We found out only a few weeks ago that Mark was being deployed again. This is his third time over there, and I thought I would be more mentally prepared, but I wasn't. He feels terrible — hates leaving us, but he's career and that's what officers do. On such short notice I was really having trouble finding someone to help out with the kids. I interviewed some people — you wouldn't believe who answers ads in the paper. When I called your boss at the deli — what's his name? Ronnie? Yes, Ronnie had nothing but wonderful things to say about you, though he was sad he was going to lose you." Julie had barely gotten the words out before she suddenly threw her hand over her mouth.

She stood, pushed back her chair and started toward the bathroom, hunched over with her other hand held tight across her stomach. She didn't make it to the toilet, though. She threw up all over the hardwood floor in the hallway. When Tulsey heard the gag and then the splash, she went around the corner, where she found Julie tiptoeing over the mess in order to make it to the toilet for the second round. Tulsey stood in the bathroom doorway.

"Are you all right?"

Julie flushed the toilet and sat back on the bathroom tile, her back against the bathtub.

"Yeah, I just … my stomach wasn't feeling that great before dinner but I thought it was because I hadn't eaten in so long." A horrified look seized her flushed face. "Oh, God, I hope it wasn't the dinner. Just what I need is for dinner to make you and the kids sick."

Tulsey pulled a soft blue hand towel off the rack next to the sink and ran it under cool water.

"Here," she handed it to Julie. "I feel fine. I'm sure it wasn't the food. Maybe you've just caught a bug or something."

Matthew appeared at the bathroom door, a curious look on his face. "Mommy?"

"Mommy's not feeling good —" Julie stopped and looked at his feet. "Is that — did you step in mommy's throw-up?" Matthew shrugged and picked up one foot, revealing a vomit-soaked sock.

"Sit, Matthew." Julie reached to pull off his socks.

"I've got it," Tulsey said. "You sit for a minute." Tulsey pulled off both of Matthew's socks. She swallowed her gags and tried to breathe through her mouth to avoid the sour smell. She sat him on the side of the tub and washed his feet. By this time, Lila was crying from her high chair in the kitchen. Tulsey navigated her way around the vomit in the hallway and picked her up.

She occupied the kids while Julie cleaned up the mess. After she helped with the dishes, she left, telling Julie to come get her if she needed help. Instead of going up to her apartment, Tulsey unlocked the door to the garage and flipped on the fluorescent light, revealing a collection of woodworking tools: handsaws, circular saws, chisels, cans of varnish, and a toolbox stuffed full of hammers, different sizes of nails and crumpled pieces of used sandpaper. Julie had agreed to give her half of the garage, which she said she hardly ever used, so Tulsey could set up a workshop. She pulled a piece of shaped wood, the leg of a stool, out from a box and took the scrap cloth cover off. She set it on her workbench and pulled up a chair, then took a piece of sandpaper out of the tool box and began to rub it over the oak, softening the surface with each stroke and pausing occasionally to blow away the sawdust.

As she worked the piece, the rhythmic motion of her hands made her thoughts drift, as they always did. It was what she loved so much about woodworking. It kept her hands busy so that her mind was free to wander. Plus, she needed a break. It had been a big day. She thought about Matthew's dirty socks and the pungent smell of vomit that emanated while she adjusted the water temperature in the bathtub so it wouldn't burn his feet. Her throat tightened again just at the thought. She saw Julie leaning her head back against the wall in the bathroom as she held the cool washrag to her forehead.

Then Tulsey drifted into recent memories of her parents. She thought about the look of crushing disappointment on their faces the night she told them at the dinner table that she was leaving Lichten. Even now, as she relived the moment, she could see the way the muscles in her father's face tensed, though he maintained a calm voice as always. He had explained that he and her mother would not be able to keep up the farm much longer. If she were to move away, he said, they would have to consider selling.

He didn't deserve to be abandoned, especially not given her mother's health. But, Tulsey reasoned, there was no other way. No other way at all. She could not stand the thought of watching her mother slip away. There was no way her close friends could really understand what it felt like to watch your mother slowly die — they didn't have to see the light and the spirit and the joy drain out of their mothers' faces like tiny grains of sand through the cinched waist of an hourglass. They didn't have to endure the cover-up: her mother's description of the disease as "a very slow progression." Her father's feigned optimism when he cheerfully summarized doctor's visits. Tulsey had to remember every day that her mother's illness had not been a nightmare, but rather was her new reality, laid down on her tired bones each morning like a smothering lead blanket before she even had the chance to climb out of bed.

An hour passed. Tulsey set down the stool leg and reached into her pocket for her cell phone. She dialed the farm. The phone rang and rang, and Tulsey cursed her parents for being too old fashioned to get an answering machine. "If they want to reach us, they'll call back or just come over," her mom had said once. They were always resisting technology. But where could they be now? It was almost 9:00 p.m. They hardly ever went out. Tulsey snapped her cell phone closed and looked at the small date glowing on the screen beneath the clock digits. June 20th. They must have gone to Siebel's for steak. Their thirty-fifth wedding anniversary. She had been so caught up in the affairs of her new life that she had forgotten to call. She leaned her head over the back of the chair, taking in the dirty intricacies of the garage ceiling before the sting of tears obscured her sight.

TWO

Brenda Dunboro, one of the two neighbors who lived across Nacre Court from the Currans, tied her satin robe, walked into the bathroom, and examined her face in the mirror. She could see three hairs sprouting between her eyebrows. She bent down beneath the sink and retrieved a small, black, waterproof bag that held all of the most undesirable grooming products she owned. She pulled out a pair of tweezers and tugged at each hair, removing them one by one. She inspected her nails and found two areas on her left forefinger and one on her right thumb where her Peach Dreams nail polish had chipped.

She pulled open the cabinet door and took out a plastic bag of cotton balls. She reached up again and took out a bottle of nail polish remover and quickly prepared her nails for a new paint job. She hadn't gotten up early enough to have time to paint her nails, but she couldn't very well let them stay the way they were either. She would just have to improvise.

"Mom?" her daughter, Laura, called. Two nails painted, Brenda put down the polish bottle and walked to her daughter's room.

"Have you showered yet?" Brenda asked.

Laura shook her head.

"You have to shower. Our guests are going to be here soon."

"Can I wear my blue dress?"

"No, honey, you need to wear the pleated skirt and your pink sweater set that we laid out last night."

"But I don't like that outfit. The skirt is dorky-looking."

"It's lovely."

Laura rolled her eyes.

"Laura, don't give me a hard time over this, please. I still have a lot to do before the brunch, and I don't have time to argue."

Brenda returned to her bathroom and pulled out her hot wax machine from beneath the old turquoise towels in the bathroom linen closet. She tore open a fresh packet of wax, dumped it in the machine and flipped the on switch. When the wax was hot, she dipped the spatula in and smeared it all over one side of her left leg. She laid one of the small white pieces of cloth carefully on her shin, pressed it down, took a deep breath and yanked. She could see little specks of black all over the other side of the cloth and though the skin beneath was red, it was so, so smooth. It didn't hurt anywhere near as much as it used to. Brenda had read in *Cosmopolitan* that repeated waxing could actually deaden the nerves in skin, so she took pleasure in thinking that in time she would no longer be bothered by it at all.

Brenda planned to wear the short, but not inappropriately short, skirt with the strawberries on it she had gotten on sale the week before at Nordstrom. She had found it on one of her coffee afternoons — that was when she bought the biggest, most complicated non-fat coffee she could find in the Valiant Crossing mall and began to search, row by row, for expensive-looking bargains. She always showed up at the mall just before it opened at 10:00. She sat in her car and listened to one song on the XM Radio classical station. She wrote the name of the composer in her day planner so she could memorize it. Classical music was by no means her favorite genre, but she felt that every educated adult should at least have some degree of familiarity with the masters. Knowledge and culture separated people like her from the people who had to work at Nordstrom.

Her first stop once inside the store was always the perfume counter, where she tried the latest designer fragrance. If she had a social event coming up, she would ask for a sample so she could wear it later, when others could enjoy the scent. No sense in keeping all that olfactory beauty to herself. She enjoyed the time-warp feeling she got from windowless department stores at the mall, and she was often pleased to discover when she walked out into the sunny day that it was nearly 3:00 p.m. and five hours had been spent.

Brenda blow-dried her dark curly hair straight and then put large hot rollers in to give it some body. Without the blow-drying, it was almost certain to frizz. She walked downstairs and retrieved the large coffee pot from the cupboard. She took out five scoops of fresh hazelnut flavored coffee beans and ground them to a fine texture in the electric grinder before she poured them into the filter. After the pot was steaming and she could smell the fresh coffee, she headed back upstairs.

She took the curlers out one by one and pulled her hair half back into a golden barrette. Three rounds of hairspray secured it. She went into Laura's room with the hairspray and brush.

"You look cute, honey."

Her daughter lifted her eyes but not her head from the pocket video game she was playing.

"Don't get an attitude with me, young lady, or you'll spend the whole party in your room. C'mon, let's do your hair." They walked to the bathroom and Brenda pulled the brush over her daughter's long, silky brown hair. She caught a snarl and Laura's head jerked back.

"We have to get out the tangles. Hold still." Having such influence over her daughter's appearance wouldn't last forever. Laura would soon be a pre-teen and start to demand that she style her own hair and choose her own clothes, which could only lead to disaster. Brenda shuddered.

When Laura's hair was finished, Brenda applied her own make-up, starting first with two applications of liquid foundation. She used a color that was a shade darker than her own skin tone because it made her look tan and diminished the appearance of her freckles. Next, she swept on bronzer, then blush in a coordinating shade of peach. She used the black eyeliner and mascara that the woman at the make-up counter at Saks had told her made her eyes really "pop," and then finished off her face with golden lip gloss.

Any minute the guests would arrive. She hurried to the kitchen and pulled a platter of fresh melon, grapes, and pineapple out of refrigerator. She had stayed up until nearly 1:00 a.m. cutting and arranging the fruit, but now the work was done and it seemed worth the effort. She peeled the plastic wrap from a tray of pastries. She had cheated and picked them up at the French bakery the day before. She also took out a pitcher of fresh-squeezed orange juice and a tray of smoked salmon, cream cheese, and bagels. Once she had set it all out on the dining room table around a bouquet of mixed summer flowers, Brenda lit two candles that sat atop small dark wooden tables in each of the room's two windows. Just as she was blowing out the second match, the doorbell rang. She swatted her hand around a few times to clear the smell of sulfur, took one final look at herself in the china cabinet mirror, put on a smile, and walked toward the front door.

In a matter of minutes, the crowd was humming happily, sharing news of their children's latest accomplishments, drinking mimosas and nibbling on baby quiche. Brenda looked out her storm glass door and saw her elderly neighbor from across the street, Louis Johnson, slowly rolling toward the front door in his red and gray motorized cart. A basket in the front looked like a mini grocery cart, and he had placed a pot of yellow mums in it. The pot bounced with each crack in Brenda's artisan crafted flagstone front path. He always brought mums to her annual neighborhood luncheon. She knew they were the cheapest thing at the grocery store that could pass as a hostess gift, and they were always dead within three days.

Behind Mr. Johnson was Warren Gloster, Brenda's next-door-neighbor, whom she had long thought to be one of the most attractive men she had ever seen. Before she could get a good look at Warren's dirty blond curls and his tan, toned arms, Brenda saw Julie Curran and her two kids, both of them total brats, walking up the sidewalk next to that odd young woman she had watched move in about a week before, the woman with the apartment full of junk and one exquisite mother of pearl antique vanity table.

Brenda opened the door. "Come on in, so nice to see you, everyone."

Mr. Johnson stood from his chair and stepped up the one stair in what looked like slow motion, then turned around painstakingly and took the mums from his basket, handing them to Brenda. "For you, Mrs. Dunboro," he grinned, showing his dentures. "Thank you for having this wonderful party. Everyone in the neighborhood looks forward to it all year."

Julie handed Lila to Tulsey and took one side of Mr. Johnson's chair as Warren took hold of the other side. They lifted it up the step and set it back down, and Mr. Johnson, looking exhausted, sat back down. Warren held the storm door open as Mr. Johnson powered his way over the seam in the doorway and into the front foyer. Brenda grimaced as she watched his wheels leave streak marks on the hardwood floor.

"Brenda, I'd like you to meet Tulsey," Julie said. "She's our new nanny and she's living in the apartment above our garage."

"Tulsey Winslow." Tulsey reached out her hand. "Nice to meet you."

Her voice was hoarse, she smelled like paint thinner, and not only was her hand thick and rough with calluses, but she shook hands with the grip of a man. She wore a dress made of the same material as thermal underwear that had been fashionable in the early 1990s, but now was not only hideously outdated, but also inappropriate for both warm and cold weather. Brenda could see that the shoulders were misshapen from where the edges of the hanger had pulled on the cotton.

"Nice to meet you. I'm Brenda. Have you met Warren and Mr. Johnson?"

Julie piped in and introduced Tulsey to the two men, then took off after Matthew, who had run to the table and was grabbing as many cookies as he could hold.

Brenda excused herself as quickly as possible to attend to the other guests, and, a while later, found herself around the corner from the punch bowl. Tulsey was chatting with Joan Carrigan, the richest old bird in the neighborhood. Brenda busied herself by refilling the crackers on the table just inside the living room so she could listen to what was sure to be an interesting exchange.

"So what do you do, dear?" Mrs. Carrigan asked Tulsey.

"I'm a nanny for Julie and Mark Curran's kids. I may also get a part-time job as a secretary."

"Oh, yes, the Currans. I have met them a number of times at Rick and Brenda's parties. Lovely people. Mark is deployed again, I've heard. Hope everything is all right with him."

Tulsey smiled and gave a hesitant nod.

"Do you have any children of your own?" Mrs. Carrigan ladled fruit punch into a crystal glass.

Tulsey shook her head.

"Then I take it you're not married, dear?"

"Not married, no."

"Not to worry. A lot of young women are waiting these days to settle down. Of course, back in my day, people were getting married a lot earlier. I was only twenty when I married Ralph." Brenda fought a smile as she listened.

"I guess some of us are just luckier than others." Tulsey cleared her throat. "Listen, it was lovely to meet you, Mrs. Carrigan. I'd better get back to Julie and the kids."

Brenda walked through the spacious dining room, delighting in the detailed crown molding she and her husband had had installed last winter. The pure white color really did coordinate with the champagne walls, just like the interior designer had promised.

She walked into the kitchen, set down her delicate antique coffee cup on its saucer, and picked up the phone to dial her husband's cell number. When he didn't answer, she looked at her watch and then out the window to see if she could see his car coming. She hung up the phone and stared briefly at the stove, her thoughts wandering to where he might be, until she heard Julie's heels click on the kitchen floor tile.

"Where's Rick?"

Brenda turned. "He had a meeting with a client this morning. You know how it is. Some of these clients want him at all hours of the day, and it's hard to turn down the cases when they're so big."

"Who's he working with this time?" Julie took a bite from a baby quiche.

"Another development company." Brenda emptied the grinds from the coffee maker and set a fresh pot to brew.

"Any new buildings going up around here I should know about?"

"More like one that already did go up — you know, that fifty-five and over community off Chestnut — and now the NIMBYs are all out in force, saying it's not what they had agreed to. Anyway, how's Mark? Have you heard from him?"

"A couple of emails," Julie's eyes shifted away from Brenda's. "He's doing all right. He's still getting set up and debriefed."

"How are you holding up? Are you nervous?"

"Lucky for me, I'm an old pro at this now," Julie put her empty plate on the countertop near the kitchen. "I'd better go make sure my children aren't terrorizing Tulsey."

"I've been meaning to ask you about Tulsey. How did you find her?" Brenda pursed her lips as she waited for Julie's response.

"Through an ad in the paper."

Brenda swallowed her coffee and lowered her voice slightly. "I know you have a lot on your plate, with Mark being away and all, but how much do you actually know about her?"

"A lot, I suppose. I interviewed her, called her references. Everything checked out." Julie's face reddened. "I wouldn't leave my children with someone I didn't trust."

Brenda no longer whispered. "Of course not. I didn't mean to — it's just that it's quite clear that she's not from around here, and anyone you bring into the neighborhood, you bring into our lives, my daughter's life, and I just wanted to be sure, you know." She shrugged and then nodded several times in rapid succession. "Just being sure. You can never be too careful these days."

Julie reached out and touched Brenda lightly on the shoulder. Her face was stricken, and Brenda was confused for a moment, trying to read her. The next moment, Julie dashed for the trash compactor, feebly pushing buttons to try to get it to open. She kicked the stainless steel front in frustration, crossed the kitchen and threw up in the sink. Brenda's eyes widened.

"Oh, God, was it — did I say too much?" Brenda took a glass from the cupboard and filled it with ice water. "I didn't mean to insinuate anything, I really ... I just," she stopped cold. "Is it the food? Is something wrong with the quiche? Oh, God, I'd better go pull the platter off the table."

Julie flipped back her hair, then took a sip from the glass and swirled the water around in her mouth, spitting in out into the sink. She turned on the faucet and flipped the switch for the garbage disposal. "It's not the food," she said over the disposal's rumble. "I haven't been feeling the greatest in the past few days. I think I may have some kind of flu. Or maybe it's stress. I don't know."

"I'm so relieved. Not relieved because you're sick — I feel terrible that you're not feeling well, but I shudder to think what would happen if I poisoned my guests."

"I'm going to go use your bathroom if you don't mind. Then I think we should probably head home."

Brenda walked to the living room and listened to a car pull up outside. She pushed away the sheer drapes and saw her husband in his

Lexus SUV. She exhaled with relief. He got out of the car and swung his suit jacket over his shoulder. She went to the front door to greet him.

"Sorry I'm late," he said to the guests. He set down his briefcase and hung his suit jacket over the closet door knob. "Had to drop in to the office this morning." Various excited greetings came from around the room, and he put his hand on Brenda's waist and kissed her on the cheek. He fixed himself a plate of food and mingled with the guests, and Brenda watched as he transitioned seamlessly from talking to one woman about her husband's cancer to another woman about her son's soccer league. He worked the room, ending conversations as smoothly as he had begun them. Brenda thought she could actually see disappointment in their guests' faces when he moved on.

She watched Rick walk upstairs, and when he did not come back down, she called up the stairs to him.

"Honey? Aren't you going to come entertain our guests?" He did not respond. She knew better than to call after him again.

***

When she got home from the Dunboros' party, Tulsey changed into shorts and pulled her desk chair onto the landing of the stairs outside. She saw that Mr. Johnson, the only black man she had seen so far in the neighborhood, was sitting outside, too, taking in the late afternoon sun on his dilapidated porch. She sat and smoked, flicking her ashes into a coffee can as she tried not to look across the court at Warren's house. He was in there somewhere now, that beautiful man she had met just a few hours before. Tulsey had tried not to be too obvious, but she had worked her way over to the seat next to his at the brunch. He was very easy to talk to, and she learned that he was a computer programmer who had bought his house in the neighborhood about five years ago. He liked to play racquetball and read science fiction, and he only went to Brenda and Rick's once a year for this very event. He didn't wear a wedding ring and there was no mention of a wife. His oval glasses were silver, his eyes blue, and he wore penny loafers with striped cotton socks. He was excruciating. Besides his good looks, he was smart, confident, educated and fairly well off — everything the men she had dated in Lichten were not.

She saw a shadow move across one of Warren's upstairs windows, and she put out her cigarette and went inside, fearing he might look out and see her peering in. She was going to turn on the television, but she realized her cell phone was blinking. She checked her messages and sat on the edge of the bed. She tried to take in Robin Marks' message. She had gotten the job; she could start in a week. She played it over again, just to make sure. She could see it all now: office happy hours with martinis and shrimp cocktail, a new crop of friends who were ambitious and accomplished, a closet full of pinstripe shirts and designer blouses and perhaps … perhaps a move to a full-time position that would pay her enough to set aside money for community college and afford her an apartment in the city.

Tulsey opened the refrigerator and cracked a can of Miller Lite. She sat on the floor, her back to the side of her bed and her knees curled up to her chest. She called her parents. When her mother answered, she could hear the loud grind of the blender in the background.

"Is dad making one of his chocolate shakes again?"

"I have no idea how one man can eat so much ice cream."

Tulsey imagined her mom sitting in the kitchen at the farm, a crossword puzzle and a cup of cold coffee on the table before her.

"He wonders why I have to keep adding new holes to expand his belt."

Tulsey laughed. "I got the secretary job, Mom. And an anniversary card is in the mail to you. I'm sorry I missed it. I tried calling, but you two must have been out to dinner."

"If a card had showed up from you, I'm not sure I would have known who you are." Something in her mother's tone hurt Tulsey.

"That's not funny, Mom." Tulsey couldn't think of anything to say. She tugged at a hangnail on her thumb until it started to bleed.

"Anyway," her mom said, "we had our usual anniversary dinner at Siebel's." Tulsey took a gulp from her beer can.

"When do you start this new job?"

"Next week."

"And they're paying you well?"

"Thirteen an hour."

"Twice what you were making at Ronnie's. Not bad. And how do you like Valiant? How's your apartment?"

"It's not as great as a place in the city would be, but this will do for now. I went to a luncheon at one of the neighbor's today. You should see this woman. She's perfect, right down to her fingernail polish. The house is huge and gorgeous. The other neighbors seem nice enough, as far as I can tell. How are things at home? Did you and Dad get the crankshaft fixed?"

"Yes, we're fine. Everything's just as it always is here, only minus you." Her mother's voice sounded hollow.

Tulsey was still thinking about that "minus you" when she took the kids out for lunch the next weekend. Julie had gotten a last minute interpreting gig, and she said she really needed the money, so Tulsey agreed to take the kids for the day. Tulsey kneeled on the floor in Matthew's room, replaying those two words over in her head while she struggled to push the boy's sneakers onto his feet. He sang the first three verses of Bingo, each with increasing volume. She tied his shoes. She turned and saw that Lila had crawled over to the dresser and was trying to pull out one of the drawers. She picked her up, causing her to scream, and took Matthew by the hand.

"Are we going to the restaurant in your car, Miss Tulsey?"

"I don't have a car."

"Why not?"

"Because I've never really needed one, and cars are very expensive."

"How do we get there, then?"

"We're going to walk. It's just outside the neighborhood and across the street. You and Lila can ride in the stroller, and I'll push. It'll be fun."

"When we go, Mommy always drives."

"I know, but today we're going to do it a little different."

Gulliver's was a bar and grill in the same shopping center as Navajo Joe's, and Julie had suggested they go there for chicken fingers and fries as a treat to make up for her being gone for the day. When they arrived at the restaurant's carved wooden front door, Tulsey lifted Matthew out of his seat and held Lila in one arm. She tried to fold up the double stroller with the other hand. She had to both pull the lever and push the button at the same time, and she shook the stroller with increasing force as much out of frustration as in an attempt to get it to fold. Fuck it, she thought, putting both kids back into it and rolling the massive Graco into the restaurant with her.

"Table for three, and two high chairs, please," she told the hostess as she tried to catch her breath.

"I don't have to sit in a high chair! I never sit in a high chair!" Matthew stomped his foot.

"You can sit in a regular chair, then."

The inside of the restaurant was dark and smelled like fried fish and vinegar. Fish and chips was the daily special, according to the colored chalk board just inside the door. A few older men sat at the bar to the side watching a baseball game and drinking beer from heavy mugs. Tulsey's feet stuck to the floor. It took a steady hand to maneuver the stroller through the narrow spaces between the tables. She parked it in the aisle next to their table and then noticed that Warren was sitting at the other end of the restaurant, having lunch with a woman. He looked in her direction, and she quickly shifted her eyes to the television mounted on the wall.

Lila played with a stuffed penguin she had brought from home, and when the server arrived, Matthew snatched it from her and Lila began to cry. Tulsey was able to speak over her for a moment, but after she had ordered their food, Lila let out a blood-curdling scream.

"Matthew," Tulsey said, "give it back to your sister."

He pretended he couldn't hear and continued playing with the toy, moving its flippers up and down and whispering to its face.

"Matthew!"

No response.

People in the restaurant started to stare, so Tulsey picked up Lila, took Matthew by the arm and walked them both outside. Matthew tried to run away from her and into the parking lot, but Tulsey, Lila dangling in her arm, grabbed him again.

"Matthew, stand still. Stand right here. You're not in trouble; I just have to get your sister to stop crying." He ran up to the front of the restaurant and leaned against the wall. He looked at Tulsey as if he might try to take off at any minute. Tulsey rubbed Lila's head, and she wiped her face with a tissue she had in her pocket. She told her she was just hungry and the food would be at the table soon. Lila's cries became more and more half-hearted.

The door to the restaurant swung open, and the woman that Warren had been with came through. She was beautiful in the sweetest of ways. Her long brown hair hung in loose spirals, freckles sprinkled her fair skin and the tip of her nose curled up. She wore loose linen pants with a T-shirt that only hinted at her feminine frame.

The woman stopped just outside the door. She held both hands to her face for a moment and let out a few soft sobs before she reached into her purse and pulled out her keys, stepping off the curb and making her way to her car.

Tulsey ushered both kids back into the restaurant and got them seated again. She saw Warren pull a few bills from his wallet and set them on the table. He walked out without acknowledging her. Maybe he didn't see her. It was a large restaurant and it was very dim inside. Or maybe he just didn't feel like talking after whatever it was that had just happened with that woman.

Her head aching, Tulsey reached to grab some aspirin from her purse, but it wasn't where she had slung it over the back of her chair. She frantically felt around on the ground, then asked the server, but no one had seen anything. Her wallet, cell phone and all the cash she had for the next week was gone. She closed her eyes. Through the darkness, she could hear Lila begin to shriek again.

THREE

"Stay behind me, Laura!" Julie heard Brenda's voice boom through the parking lot of the community club house.

"Okay, Mom." Julie heard Laura drag out the phrase in annoyance. She watched the two of them carry grocery bags and a large silver coffee pot into the front door. Brenda was always in charge, or at least always made herself in charge, of refreshments for the Gemstone Terrace Homeowners Association meetings. Julie thought she always went overboard. She thought some bottled water would do. It was nice to have something to snack on, though, since the meeting sometimes dragged on for three hours or longer. The boredom factor was insignificant when compared to the benefit of being around other adults for occasional chit chat. This particular evening, Julie was especially glad to have time away from the kids. It was Tulsey's night to have them, and rather than hole up in her room to sleep or read or watch a movie, Julie thought it would be best if she got out.

She sat in the second row and looked on as Brenda began arranging in lines on a platter the peanut butter sandwich cookies she had brought. Brenda smoothed out the rows by running the palm of her hand along the edges of the rows until the cookies lined up just so. She stacked plastic cups and poured a mixture of Sprite and fruit punch into a large bowl, then finished it off with a scoop of lime sherbet on top. She had actually brought a tub of lime sherbet and an ice cream scooper. Julie bit back a smirk. Just watching Brenda was exhausting, but a small part of Julie would have done anything in that moment to have just a fraction of Brenda's daily energy — even if it was fueled by an unnaturally strong need to be perfect in every way.

Even Brenda's make-up was exquisite. Julie stared at her as she stacked up Styrofoam coffee cups. The lines she had painted around her eyes followed her lids seamlessly, as if they had been tattooed on. Maybe they were tattooed on. Some ladies were doing that now. Brenda's skin was completely free of any freckles or blemishes, and there wasn't a speck of shine to be seen. Her blackened eyelashes gently curled up, accentuating her almond-shaped eyes. The plum stain on her lips glistened in the fluorescent light. She had to have gone to beauty school, or perhaps some expensive Mary Kay week-long tutorial, to have learned to apply make-up that way.

"Hi, Julie, it's nice to see you," Warren said as he walked past and sat down toward the back of the room.

Julie smiled and gave a small nod.

The Homeowners Association Board members, including Rick, filed into the fluorescent light one by one, with wrinkled shirts and bothered hair from their long days at work. Brenda set up the nameplates for the officers at the head table. She took just a moment longer arranging her husband's name plate, which read "Rick Dunboro, President," than she did on the others. The Wilkinsons were there, of course. They were both retired and hadn't missed a meeting in probably five years. About forty people showed up and the chattering got increasingly louder until Rick broke it with his commanding voice.

"Members of the Gemstone Terrace Homeowners Association, this meeting is officially called to order."

The board spent the first forty-five minutes taking comments from members on whether the new $30,000 performance pavilion, which was a glorified platform with a tent as far as Julie could tell, should be built parallel or perpendicular to the south side of the pool. Five members were worried about noise from summer folk concerts projecting all the way to their homes, so they advocated for the perpendicular placement. Not everyone liked live music, and they were entitled to some peace and quiet on weekend evenings, Mrs. Lankin argued.

But several other members thought that building it perpendicular would not be in keeping with the pool and clubhouse design, which was clean and balanced.

"Why would we want a pavilion awkwardly jutting out into the green space when the length of the pool fence can accommodate the back of the pavilion perfectly," Mr. Wilson asked. Weatherstone had built their pavilion parallel to their pool and it looked fabulous, he said.

After everyone had had their say and Mr. Wilson had accused Mrs. Lankin of having a "rowdy" barbecue the summer before that had been severely disturbing to him and his family, Rick announced that the board would vote on the issue at next month's meeting.

"All right, on to the proposed neighborhood ordinances," Rick said. "Betty Frank has put forth a resolution that would disallow anyone to have the vehicles in their driveway blocking the sidewalk. We had discussion on this at last month's meeting, so all we need to do tonight is vote. Do I have a motion?"

"A motion to approve the resolution allowing the board to issue citations to all residents who leave their cars blocking the sidewalk," Betty Frank said.

"Do I have a second?" Rick asked.

"Second," two board members said at once.

"All right, all those in favor say aye."

Five board members said aye.

"All those opposed," Rick said.

"Nay," three board members said.

"Ordinance passes five to three," Rick said. "Beginning on the first of next month, anyone who is found with their car blocking the sidewalk or overlapping it in any way will be fined $30. The money will go into the association's general fund. Before we adjourn, does anyone have any comments they want to make before the board?"

"Is that pothole on Topaz going to be fixed soon? I popped my tire on it last week," Bob Cleavy asked.

"Phyllis, as our transportation chair, do you want to answer that?"

Phyllis was an older woman with a smart gray bob and black-rimmed glasses. She was probably a nice woman, but Julie was slightly afraid of her because she looked so much like the evil librarian that had worked at her junior high school back in the day.

"Yes, the county is planning to come on Friday to fill it in," she said sternly. "And I will call them tomorrow to make sure that's still their plan."

"Anyone else?" Rick asked. No one raised a hand. "Then before we go, I have a concern to put before the board. Mr. Johnson at 4024 Nacre Court — across the street from us — has not been taking care of his yard." The room was silent for a moment and then Bonnie Byers, who lived all the way across Gemstone Terrace from Nacre Court, brushed her long, wavy curls off her shoulder and raised her hand.

"I saw dozens of dandelions in his lawn when I was over there the other week visiting the Dunboros," she said. "And I'm pretty sure he has a dead bush out front."

"More than just one," Rick said. "He leaves his trash can and recycling bin out a day — sometimes even two — after pick-up. It looks terrible."

Julie half-raised her hand, then raised it all the way when it looked like Rick was not going to call on her to speak.

"He's an aging man, and, considering his limited mobility, I think he's doing a pretty decent job at keeping up his yard," she said.

"What if he just can't *do* any more than he's doing to keep the place up?" Warren asked from his seat without waiting to be called on. "Or what if he just likes it the way it is? It's his property. I live across from him, too, and it doesn't bother me."

"We have a superior set of standards for lawn appearance in this neighborhood," Bill Albertson said from his seat at the board's table. "Our residents should want to keep their properties looking their absolute best. It's a matter of pride, and a matter of property values."

"I take it you've seen his yard, then," Rick asked Bill.

"Not yet, but I've heard about it, and I intend to drive by it tomorrow and take a look," Bill said. "At any rate, it seems like there's enough concern to issue a warning letter."

"I agree," Rick said, "and if it's not improved by out next meeting, we can discuss issuing a citation. And another thing, I would like to propose that in the next meeting we discuss a motion to require that he remove the two trees on the side of the pond."

"The ones in Mr. Johnson's yard?" Julie asked. "What's the matter with them? Do they have that fungus that's been going around?"

"No," Rick said. "They've grown so large that no one else on Nacre Court can see the golf course pond."

There was a fire in Julie that she didn't recognize.

"I can see the pond just fine," she said.

"I've asked him to trim them back, but he hasn't done anything about it," Rick went on, pretending not to have heard her. "And to be honest, I think they may actually be on land that the HOA owns."

"They're stunning trees, some sort of magnolia, I believe," Julie said.

Rick cleared his throat and began organizing and packing away his papers.

"I'll check into it and we can revisit the issue at the next meeting. Would anyone else like to raise any issues before we finish up?"

The crowd was quiet.

"Meeting adjourned."

When Julie got home, she quickly kissed Lila and Matthew on the forehead, then asked Tulsey if she wouldn't mind staying for another half hour or so.

"I would love to be able to take a bath before I have to put the kids down," she told Tulsey.

Tulsey obliged.

Julie grabbed a beer from the fridge and snapped off the cap, sucking down the foam that erupted from the top so it wouldn't end up on the kitchen floor. She went upstairs and turned on the bathroom light. She pushed the rubber stopper into the drain and watched absently as the water collected. The condensation from the outside of the bottle ran together below her thumb and collected into a frigid drop that splattered when it hit her knee. She looked down at the wet spot on her leg and thought about wiping it away, but did not.

Instead, she got on her knees and dug through the toilet paper rolls and extra bottles of lotion in the cupboard under the sink. She pulled out the pregnancy test she had thrown into her cart three days ago at the grocery store. She hadn't bought it thinking there was any chance she were pregnant, but she was nauseated and a two-pack was on sale and she thought she'd better check. Had the tests not been on sale, she probably wouldn't have bought them at all.

What if I am? The words were so loud in her head that she swore if someone else had been in the room they would have heard them, too. The sound of the flowing water was a good cover-up, if not for the voice in her head, then for the time she would need to be upstairs to await the result. What if I am? There it was again. Had she actually said it aloud? She wasn't sure.

When she bought the pregnancy test, she'd tried to regard it as no different from a can of peas. A household item. A toiletry, if you will. Just another item on the list.

She was alone with the thing now. She could feel the heat from the recessed lighting pounding the back of her neck. Her upper lip began to bead with sweat so she licked her lips, letting in the warm taste of salt. She tore open the plastic and carefully rolled the packaging in toilet paper so there was no chance of it being noticed, then threw it into the blue wicker wastebasket next to the sink. She took one more sip of beer and sat on the toilet, holding the test between her legs.

When she was satisfied that it had been saturated, she carefully placed the stick on the thin edge of the sink. She would have to wait three minutes before she could be sure. Please let it be only one line. Only one line. She sat back on the toilet, her chin in her hands, her bare toes tapping silently on the floor tiles.

Julie had peed on a stick many times before, though never with an open beer perched on the back of the toilet. When she and Mark had started trying to get pregnant, she took one every month, sometimes even before her period was supposed to have started. It was always a time of delicious anxiety. When the test came back positive for Matthew, she and Mark had had celebratory sex, after which Mark brought her a dinner of fish sandwiches from Long John Silver's.

Her husband had made her a dozen chocolate pecan cookies every week for the first four months of that pregnancy. She had been sick in the mornings but had an insatiable desire for sweets in the evenings. Those same cookies became Matthew's favorite as soon as he was old enough to have dessert.

After Lila was born, Julie had decided to cut way back on her hours at work. Her mother had been a stay-at-home mom with her and her brother, and Julie felt she owed it to her children to be home with them as much as she could. It was lonely at first, and the days seemed to drag. Julie joined the Family Readiness Group on post, which was forty-five minutes from Valiant. There, she and the other military wives talked about life as single mothers. She came to recognize, though, that those early mornings when she sat rocking her red-faced, sweet-smelling babies until they fell back asleep were precious moments in her life to which nothing else would ever quite compare.

That landscape of contentment had given way to some new, strange, undiscovered wilderness some months ago. It hadn't happened over a long period of time, as Julie had previously thought all changes in family life did. Instead, it came down upon her in loads. Her heavy sadness coordinated with Mark's deployments, each one worse than the previous. This, the third, had left her alone yet again, too overwhelmed in all regards to handle the affairs of the home and the family on her own. She had always thought mothers who hired nannies were weak or lazy or selfish. Here she was now, even with Tulsey's help, barely able to manage.

And her husband — the one who would lie awake for an hour, having lost feeling in his arm entirely because she had fallen asleep on his shoulder — was scarcely different from the neighbor Rick Dunboro, whom Julie would hear pulling into his driveway at ten o'clock each night. Mark had told her that his traveling with the Army would not dominate their lives. He pointed out other military families who seemed to be together all the time.

He had no way of knowing there would be such a long war, Julie thought. He was an optimist, and surely he had hoped for the best for all of them. Now he didn't have any choice. His career was with the Army. No other job would take care of them the way this did. Mark was just going through, day by day, battling like everyone else to keep going, to keep getting up in the morning, to keep paying bills, to keep getting closer to that blessed day when he had done enough, been enough, earned enough to set his life on cruise control.

Mark had always been an adventurer, much more so than Julie, who liked the calm and the predictable and who always preferred a glass of wine and a movie in to a trip to a flashy restaurant or a weekend away in a rustic cabin. They were young when they married, Julie reminisced, still tapping her toes on the bathroom floor. So young and so in love that there was no way she would have — could have — forbidden him from joining the Army. It seemed an inevitability. The job that would give purpose to his life. The job that brought with it the rewards of camaraderie and identity as much as salary. The sacrifice wouldn't be all his. He was squeezing out two lives without being in two places at once. Matthew and Lila still kissed his face, jumped into his arms when he came home.

The night before Mark left, he had come to Julie in their bedroom, reaching up the sleeve of her silk robe to caress her arm. He pushed his fingers between hers and led her to their bed. There was a tightness in her stomach as they made love that night. She was still attracted to him. She rubbed her hands over the muscles just beneath his hip bones as she always did. It was her favorite part of him. His blue eyes were still as attentive as always. The sinking feeling was not the kind that came from lack of arousal. As Julie considered that night more carefully, she realized the discomfort was a familiar feeling – one she had felt when she lost her virginity to Ryan Staterly in eleventh grade. One she had felt when she had sex with Mark before they were married. There was some shame about being what her mother would call a ruined woman, but mostly it was fear. Fear that her lust would lead to pregnancy. Fear that she would have a baby at a time when she could not be a good mother.

Julie reached out to the edge of the sink and clasped the plastic stick between her thumb and forefinger, bringing it close. With two silent red lines, it screamed to her what she already knew to be true: a third baby was on the way.

***

Tulsey checked the clock on the bottom of her computer screen. It read 1:00 p.m. Three more hours until quitting time. She stood up and stretched. She straightened her skirt and sat back down, one leg folded beneath her, the other dangling down. She reached into her purse and pulled out her lip balm, smearing it generously across her flaking lips. The phone rang.

"Good morning, Shaw Marketing," Tulsey said. Though she said it a hundred times a day, Tulsey sometimes came out with the wrong greeting when she lifted the receiver to her ear.

"Good afternoon," the man said with a snap. "Is Trish Shaw available?"

"No, I'm sorry, she's in a meeting," Tulsey said. "May I take a message and have her get back to you?"

"Sure, tell her to call Shmarnes Smazney."

Tulsey focused on getting down the number, and before she realized it, the hummingbird on the other end of the line was gone. Shmarnes Smazney? Tulsey thought. Oh, shit. That can't be right.

"So what you're telling me is now I have to call this number and ask who there left a message for me?" Trish said five minutes later, a fat vein appearing in her forehead.

"Sorry, Trish, he sounded like he was in a rush." Trish put up her hand, looked at her computer and put on her earpiece in one motion, all the while shaking her head.

"Hello? Shmarnes?" Tulsey heard Trish say from behind her closed office door.

As soon as Tulsey got back to her desk, Robin Marks, who had been telling Tulsey for weeks that she really needed her help with a "critical organizational project," was waiting for her. Tulsey thought this meeting might be a gesture of appreciation, a delegation of more authority to her because she had proven herself over the last two months. She had done everything asked of her well — damn near perfect, actually. She had learned how to word process, had upped her typing speed to fifty words per minute, and had mastered the quirks of the printer and copier. She had even figured out that she could fax exactly two sheets of paper – not three or the machine would jam – at a time, which, as far as she could tell, was something that even Trish Shaw herself had not learned. Tulsey had answered the phones and been courteous to every rushed, arrogant jackass who had to leave a message. Everyone calling for Trish had to leave a message; it was company policy. Trish had said it was because she never liked to talk on the phone without first preparing for the conversation, but Tulsey knew it was a ploy to make Trish look more in demand than she actually was.

Tulsey's breath quickened with anticipation as she looked at Robin's lips, waiting to see how they moved, what words they began to form, what she would tell Tulsey was her next, more demanding role.

"Oh, I'm just so glad to have you around, Tulsey. Really just so glad. I have been so busy these last few months and I haven't been able to keep up with some of my work. I'm hoping you'll help me out."

Tulsey cleared her throat and folded her hands together on the reception desk.

"Great. I'd love to," she said. "Should I come back to your office?"

"Uh, nope. No, you don't need to do that. I'll just bring the work to you so you don't miss any calls up here." With that, Robin disappeared and returned with five long boxes loaded on her stick-thin forearms. She set them all at Tulsey's feet and opened up the first box. It was filled with thousands of cleared checks, some rolled in balls, some haphazardly put in piles, others torn nearly to shreds.

"I'm going to need you to put these in numerical order," Robin said.

"How many are there?"

"In this first group? About forty-five hundred."

"Oh. Okay. And how many groups are there?"

"Five. Now, Tulsey, you're a very important part of this team. I want you to know that. You may see this as tedious work, but believe me, it's critical. Having excellent records is the key to keeping those goddamned predatory auditors at bay." Her face twitched ever so slightly as she said it, and she pulled a piece of hair that had gotten stuck in her lip gloss back from her face.

Tulsey waited until Robin left the room to let out a befuddled, albeit muffled, moan. She checked her watch. This was going to be a while. Maybe putting the checks in order would make the time go faster. She hoisted the first box onto the desk and began picking through the checks with her fingers. The checks had a subtle, light green pattern of diamonds as the background. In the upper left hand corner, they read Shaw Marketing, Inc., 1 Somerset Tower, Suite 714. The font was formal, plain, boring. In the bottom right hand corner was a stamp of Trish Shaw's signature. Patricia M. Shaw, CEO. The "S" was much larger than any of the other letters and had a loop on one end that was exaggerated and self-important.

There were checks to employees, checks to the cleaning company, checks to Daisy's Interior Design, checks to the IT consultants and a check for $10,000 to — the rat! — Mark Feinberg, the sleaziest of all the higher-ups at Shaw. Must have been a bonus, Tulsey speculated. Or hush money to keep their affair quiet. Gross. A bonus, it was a performance bonus. Tulsey giggled to herself when she thought of the word "performance." Better get to it or you'll be organizing these checks for the rest of your life, she told herself.

Check 2014, check 3560, check 2230, check 1457. She pulled out 1457 and put it at the front of the box followed by 2014, 2230 and 3560. Next it was 1365, 798, 971 and 1540. She stuffed check 1540 between 1457 and 2014 and 1365 between 1457 and 2014. Wait, was that right? She pulled the check out again and looked at the numbers. They all seemed to be switching up on her like an evil magic puzzle. Damn it. She'd start with 798 and 971 — they had to go before all the others. That much she knew. The numbers game got faster as the hours went on. She decided to take the checks out of the boxes and make piles categorized by the first digit. She could then attack each pile one at a time and the ordering would go much faster. By the time she was to leave for the day, Tulsey had ordered almost one quarter of a box. There would be fill-ins, of course, as the checks were not in perfect sequence, but she could see how far she had come. She reached down and pinched the tight stack of ordered checks between her thumb and middle finger, the feel of which made her break a half-smile. Being a critical member of a team was exhausting. So was boredom.

As soon as Tulsey got home, she lay on her bed and closed her eyes. She awoke to the sound of a knock at her screen door. She looked over and saw a figure, and as she started to come awake, she realized she had fallen asleep across her bed wearing only her button-down shirt, underwear, and panty hose. When she realized her state of undress, she squinted to see who it was.

"Looks like it was a tough day at the office," Julie said as she came through the door and stepped over the skirt and heels Tulsey had shed on the floor.

"I must have fallen asleep watching the news," Tulsey said. "How embarrassing." She opened the bottom drawer of her dresser and took out a pair of sweatpants. She put them on over her nylons, which made her legs begin to sweat. "The kids asleep?"

Julie nodded. She cautiously pulled the desk chair out and sat down. Tulsey wasn't familiar with the look on Julie's face. Not tired or concerned or happy or angry. Rather, it was bland. Like a pale bowl of grits, left out so long it had cooled and stiffened. But she wasn't immediately alarmed because, she reasoned, she didn't know Julie all that well yet. She didn't know her ins and outs the way she knew her best friend Monica's. She had known Monica since second grade. She could tell what her face looked like over the phone.

"I need to ask a favor," Julie said. Her hands were folded on her lap and she looked Tulsey in the eyes.

"Sure," Tulsey said, shrugging.

"I need you to take the day off on Thursday — I'll pay you more than what you'd make at the office to make up for it. I'm going to leave the kids with Brenda. She's usually home during the day. I'll tell her it's an emergency. I'll play sick in the morning so the kids think I have the flu. Then I'll tell them you're taking me to the doctor."

"Okay," Tulsey nodded slowly, half-expecting Julie to say she needed a girl's day out, filled with shopping and trip to the bar for some pink cocktails.

"And then I would like you to take me to the abortion clinic on Sandstone Road, you know, out past that ugly neighborhood with all those houses built in the sixties." She pointed her hand out to the left as she said it, like she had some sort of compass that allowed her to understand exactly how the eagle flies from the Curran house to this clinic.

Tulsey sat heavy in her chair. This wasn't the first time someone had made such a request. When Monica first learned she was pregnant, she had asked Tulsey to do a similar favor. In the few days leading up to the appointment, Monica had changed her mind.

But Monica's life was different. The father didn't want her to have the baby, and even if he was willing to contribute financially, he didn't have much to give. He was a handy-man who did more drugs than he did fixing. Julie, on the other hand, had a loving husband, a house, enough money and two beautiful, healthy children. Could she be having an affair? Was it her business to ask?

"It's Mark's," Julie said.

"I don't ... I wasn't ..."

"Well, I'd be wondering if I were you, so I thought I'd just get it out in the open."

"Okay," Tulsey said. It was probably true. Julie was always home with the kids, and when she wasn't, she was translating. One of Tulsey's co-workers at Shaw was married to another translator who worked with Julie and often mentioned that his wife had seen Julie at a gig.

"I just don't want another child," Julie said.

"Fair enough," Tulsey said. She hadn't really ironed out her beliefs on abortion, but Tulsey knew one thing for sure: it wouldn't be right for her to deny Julie this intimate request. Tulsey would be a good friend. It wasn't her responsibility to decide whether this was right or wrong. People have reasons — hundreds of reasons all at once — for doing what they do on any given day. And besides, maybe Julie would change her mind in the coming days, just as Monica had.

FOUR

Julie's eyes shifted around her bedroom in the soft pre-dawn light. The fan above her head spun steadily, throwing puffs of cool wind onto her face. The air felt good. Her face was damp; she must have perspired in her sleep. She looked at the dirty clothes spilling out of her hamper and into piles on the floor. The door to the bathroom was half ajar, leaving a slice of blackness to stand watch over the room. The frame with Psalm 23 in it that Mark's mother had given them had been knocked sideways – probably by Matthew when he hid from her next to the dresser in a game of hide and seek a few days before.

Her clock read 5:17. She wanted it to be any morning other than the one it was.

She couldn't believe she had slept as soundly as she had and then, as if upon command, had awakened more than an hour before her alarm was to go off. She imagined she had subconsciously willed this to happen so that she didn't risk waking the children with the alarm. She would now have plenty of time to orchestrate her bout with the "flu."

She took a glass of water, a bottle of Tylenol, and a thermometer from her bathroom cabinet and set them on her nightstand. She pulled several tissues out from the tissue box on Mark's nightstand, crumpled them up and dropped them across the bed and on the floor. She clicked on the television and tried to focus on the morning news.

She had planned it all out. The kids would awake to find their mother still in bed, sick. Tulsey would come over in the morning and call Brenda to see if she could take the kids for a couple of hours while Tulsey took Julie to the doctor's office for an emergency visit. Tulsey would explain that Julie was vomiting all over the place, and it would be too much for her to try and manage Julie and the kids. Then, Tulsey and Julie would drive to the clinic and return with a diagnosis of the flu and the perfect excuse for Julie to lay low for a couple of days. No one would be wise to her situation, especially not her kids.

At about 6:30, Matthew walked into her room, mumbling and rubbing his eyes. The back of his hair stood on end and one leg of his blue pajama pants was stuck up around his knee.

"Mommy, can I get into bed with you?" he asked. Julie wanted space, but still she instinctually held up the comforter, then curled her body around him.

"Mommy's not feeling good this morning," she told him. "Her tummy is upset." She rubbed her hand over her face and then forced out a cough.

Matthew turned to look at her and laid his head back down on the pillow. During the day, he was always so busy trying to be a big boy, but this morning, as with many mornings, he was still too tired to fight his own sweet vulnerability. His blue eyes looked at her quizzically, as though a serious question were about to come from his tiny lips.

"Can we watch cartoons?" he said instead.

"Sure," Julie said, switching the channel and nestling her arm around him.

As promised, Tulsey let herself in at 7:00 and walked upstairs to Lila's room. She lifted her out of the crib and carried her into Julie's bedroom.

"I got your message that you weren't feeling well," Tulsey said. Matthew sat up. "Maybe we should go to the doctor."

"You know, Miss Tulsey, I think maybe you're right."

Julie got up and walked, slightly hunched over, to the dresser, where she retrieved gray sweatpants and a large T-shirt. She pulled on her sneakers and explained to Matthew and Lila that she needed some medicine to make her feel better. The rest of the plan worked. Brenda was home and agreed to take the kids. Julie insisted on driving.

"I don't, um," Tulsey started as Julie put the minivan into gear, "I don't mean to be nosey but I was just wondering if you've talked to Mark."

"Talked to Mark," Julie said matter-of-factly as she stared at the road. "Talked to Mark about this?"

Tulsey nodded. "Yes," she said quietly. "I mean, I know it's none of my business and you don't have to— "

"No," Julie said shortly.

"Why not?"

Julie couldn't believe Tulsey had the nerve to question her, but now wasn't the time to alienate the one person who knew her secret. Tulsey hadn't shown any judgment thus far, so perhaps she wasn't asking for any reason other than pure curiosity. She looked over at Tulsey.

"Because I already know what he'd say."

Tulsey nodded slowly. "Makes sense," she said.

Julie said nothing while they waited at the many stoplights on the way. Bright sunlight shone down on the streets of Valiant, making everything look exaggerated and caricature-like. She half expected to see a circus clown waving from the drive-through at Kentucky Fried Chicken. The moment seemed unreal, like some kind of dream from which she would soon awake, free of the weight of a choice between bad and worse.

Julie pulled into the parking lot and was relieved to see that the office was discreet. If young women with hairy armpits and old men with Bibles did tend to hang around the entrance with homemade signs, they had gone on hiatus.

She had seen clinics portrayed in movies before, and that was all she had to go on. She had never taken a friend, never been asked to take a friend. She knew a couple of women who had had abortions, but she hadn't asked them the details. It hadn't struck her as appropriate conversation. It seemed to be difficult enough as it was for those women without any extra questions.

She was neither surprised nor expectant of what she saw when Tulsey twisted the scratched metal knob and opened the wooden door that led to the waiting room. There was a sliding glass reception window that was open, revealing an older woman with tightly curled caramel-gray hair and thick, brass-rimmed glasses. She smiled as Julie approached and signed her name on the purple sign-in sheet.

There were three other women in the waiting area. One was young and had gelled, curly dark brown hair that she twisted around her forefinger as she rapidly flipped through a copy of *People* magazine. Another was an overweight woman with blond hair and thick ankles. She had one leg crossed over another, and she jiggled the loose foot rhythmically. She had her arm linked through the almond-skinned arm of the third woman.

Julie started to list in her head, not on purpose nor by accident, the conditions in her life that mandated this decision. My children deserve to have a mother who is not overwhelmed, a mother who is present when she is with them, rather than thinking twelve steps ahead about dinner and laundry and whether the park will open on Monday evening. They deserve a mother who is not angry. I do not have time to be sick for three months straight, the way I was with both previous pregnancies. No Mark around to hold them or corral them when I get so big I can barely walk. Going from two children to three might as well be going from two to twelve. Pandemonium. All the time.

Mark could be deployed again. And again. And again. And I don't have the training to get a decent-paying job. It's already not worth it for me to work full-time because I don't make enough to cover what I'd have to pay in daycare expenses. Three kids would cement me to the house forever.

She looked down at her fingers and began carefully peeling the top layer of one thumbnail with the other, chipping it away in little bits of dandruff-like snow that fell onto the belly of her black T-shirt. It was a nervous habit she'd developed as a child, and now, at this most pivotal moment, it offered her some solace by giving her something else — anything else — to focus on.

Tulsey sat beside her, quietly chewing her own thumbnail and looking over every couple of minutes.

"You okay?" she asked once.

Julie nodded.

When the nurse came to the door, clipboard in hand, to call her back, Julie felt a force field guiding her up out of the chair and through the door. It was a powerful, yet empty determination with which she soldiered into the room, undressed, covered herself in the paper robe and eventually lay down on the table, placing her feet in the cold steel stirrups.

When she felt the sting of the syringe going in to numb her, her consciousness pulled in and she focused only on the physical sensations. She stared straight ahead, listening to the clanging of the instruments as the doctor and nurse maneuvered around her. The pressure in her uterus waxed and waned until suddenly, too suddenly, the doctor stood up and said, "We're all done."

She heard the words as though they were murmurs, shimmering their way down a long metal tube before finally exploding into her ears.

***

Sunday was the first day Julie felt up to taking care of the kids on her own. Tulsey was eager to get out and do something, anything where she didn't have to have the kids hanging all over her. Julie seemed to be doing all right, all things considered, but Tulsey nonetheless needed a break from the emotion that seemed to be oozing from the walls.

She decided to check out Navajo Joe's. It was within walking distance, she had never been there, and it had to be at least somewhat unique, as it was the only non-chain coffee shop Tulsey passed on her bus ride to work. As she made her way through the neighborhood, she saw a handful of workmen lifting a large black and gold metal fence into place around a small yellow house on Topaz Street. It had to be more than six feet tall, the kind of fence with spiky iron arrowheads at the top of each stake. Strange, she thought. It looked like the fences she had seen once around the Vice President's house on a sixth-grade field trip to Washington, D.C. This house was a Cape Cod, probably a three-bedroom, possibly a four-bedroom, smallish in comparison to other houses in Gemstone Terrace. This fence was a homeowner's penis pump.

A copper wind chime attached to the door at Navajo Joe's sang when she opened the door, announcing her arrival to the room full of people transfixed by their laptops, noshing on scones. Behind the counter was a tall man wearing a Native American headdress, feathers and all. He had silver and turquoise rings on every finger. He was as blond as blond got, with light blue eyes to match.

Tulsey considered the options: Lakota Latte, Cherokee Chai, Mohawk Mocha. She settled on a coffee of the day — hazelnut — which was the only option less expensive than an entire fast food meal. On her way to the cream and sugar bar, she thought she caught Warren out of the corner of her eye. She didn't check to make sure, though, for fear she'd make awkward eye contact. Instead, she just enjoyed the sensation of her back burning as she imagined him looking at her.

The moment was broken when Tulsey remembered that her pants were really too tight and probably allowed Warren and the rest of the coffee shop to see every agonizing cellulite dimple in her butt cheeks. She quickly snapped the plastic top onto her cup and headed to a table to sit down and read.

When it wasn't too obvious, she sneaked a glance over at the good-looking blond, but soon realized that he was, at most, high school age. Not every guy with curly hair and glasses is Warren Gloster. She leaned back in the plush purple chair and flipped open *Demons and Dragons*, the third and latest installment in a fantasy epic series in which a futuristic Achilles battles his way through the forces of darkness to find the cure to a deadly epidemic. It was good reading. Just one thing wrong, just one thing needed to fix it, and just the right hero for the job.

Twenty-some minutes later, when she looked up from the book and glanced around, the real Warren Gloster was sitting a few seats away, sipping from a thick mug. He held a paperback up to his face, and Tulsey squinted to try and make out the title. It was the first book of the same series she was reading. She stood up and straightened her pants, then slung her purse over her shoulder and walked over to him.

"Looks like you've got good taste in books," she said, brandishing hers. "Or bad taste, whichever way you want to look at it."

Warren pushed his glasses up on his face with his forefinger.

"Hi," he said, clearly taken off guard.

This was a bad idea. This is hideously awkward. But what's this guy's deal? He's never had a neighbor talk to him in a coffee shop before?

"Tulsey," she said. "We met at Rick and Brenda's luncheon." Besides, if she didn't try to get to know him now, she might lose the chance for months. She noticed his car was gone before she awoke every morning, and it often came back after she was already in her pajamas. Was it weird that she knew that? Maybe she was "noticing" him too closely.

"Ah, yes. Brenda's luncheon mostly, if memory serves," Warren said. "Nice to see you."

Conversation commenced. Nicely done, she thought. She took a seat next to him.

"So, is this the neighborhood hangout?" she asked, smiling. She set her cup on the table and pulled her purse off her shoulder.

"Nope, but it's mine," Warren said. "There is no neighborhood hangout. With the exception of HOA meetings, I usually only talk to neighbors when Brenda has her parties."

"HOA?" Tulsey asked.

"Homeowners Association meetings," Warren said. "You know, where the neighborhood spies bitch about potholes and gang up on old men."

Tulsey looked at Warren quizzically.

"This last one, Rick decided to pick on Mr. Johnson because of his yard."

"He's in a wheelchair, for Chrissakes. And his yard looks fine."

"Doesn't bother me – never has. Though it has gotten progressively more overgrown," Warren said.

"So, what, are they going to arrest him?"

"They'll fine him if he doesn't clean it up, or pay someone to clean it up. You know, cut the grass and trim the trees and all that. Sounds like Rick wants him to get rid of those two trees closest to the golf course pond. Says it's blocking his view."

"Of the muck pond?" Tulsey said, raising an eyebrow.

Warren laughed. "Yep."

"Well," Warren said, draining his mug, "I'm sorry to cut this short, but I've got to meet a friend for a racquetball game."

"Glad I ran into you," Tulsey said.

"Me, too. Now I can say I actually kind of know one of my neighbors." He smiled, revealing white teeth that were slightly crooked. "Did you drive?"

"Nah, I walked over," Tulsey said. "Needed the exercise."

"Want a ride back?" he asked.

"That'd be great." Tulsey's stomach tightened when she stood up.

Warren's car looked and smelled like he had just driven it off the BMW lot. There were no fingerprints or dog nose smears on the windows, and the carpeting had scarcely a grain of dirt on it. There was no trinket hanging from the rearview, no pine tree air freshener dangling from an air vent adjustment knob. Come to think of it, there were no signs that anyone actually drove the car, except for the half-full water bottle sitting in the cup holder. The navigation system greeted him by name when he turned the key in the ignition. Tulsey got in and snapped her seatbelt. They pulled out and came to a stop at a red light just outside the parking lot entrance.

"You from Valiant originally?"

"No. God, no," Warren said. "Colorado. Moved out here for a job after grad school. No one in Valiant is from Valiant. Except for maybe Mr. Johnson. I hear he's been in that house by himself for more than thirty years. His house was there before any of this came up," he said, loosely scanning the horizon with one hand.

"Did he ever have family?"

"Wife and a daughter. Both died of breast cancer within two years of each other."

"Jesus," Tulsey said.

Warren nodded.

"He's a fighter, I suppose." The light turned green and Warren shifted and accelerated across the intersection. "He had a stroke a few years back. That's what put him in the chair."

"How do you know so much about Mr. Johnson if you never talk to anyone in the neighborhood?" Tulsey asked.

"He had me over for dinner a couple of months ago. He just came out with it, like he hadn't talked to anyone in a while and just needed to get it out."

Tulsey nodded knowingly. "Does he have any other family?"

"I don't know," Warren said. "If he does, they're never around."

They pulled onto their court and Tulsey turned her head to look at the street sign. "Nacre Court," she read it aloud. "I've been dying to ask someone what the hell nacre is. And why did our street get such a lame name? Anyway, aren't all the roads supposed to be named after gemstones? Couldn't we just live on Diamond Court?"

"Funny you should ask," Warren said. He pulled into his driveway and put the car into park. "I looked it up before I bought my house."

Tulsey smiled and rolled her eyes.

"I just wanted to make sure it didn't mean something terrible. Color me anal."

"You said it, not me," Tulsey grinned.

"Anyway, it's the stuff that oysters put around sand grains that get inside their shells. They build it up layer by layer until they've made a pearl."

"Awesome. Our court is named after a tumor."

"I kind of like that it's not so cliché," Warren said.

"I'm just joking. It is kind of a romantic idea."

"What?" Warren said, cocking his head.

"Something painful being made into something beautiful."

"Never thought of it quite like that," Warren said. "But, yeah, I suppose it is a romantic idea. They could have just named it Pearl Court and called it a day." He looked over at Tulsey, his blue eyes lighting up beneath his glasses. She swallowed hard and grabbed for the door handle.

"Thanks for the ride," she said, stepping out onto the driveway.

"If you ever want to have, you know, a neighborly get-together, you know where to find me," Warren said.

"Let me give you my cell phone number," Tulsey said, digging through her purse for a pen. "I've got one now. I mean, again. My old one was in the purse that was stolen at Gulliver's.

"I hate that place," Warren said.

She scribbled the number on an old receipt, using her knee as a surface, and brushed off a few stray pieces of tobacco before handing it over to him.

"Great," Warren said. "I'll talk to you soon."

The words made Tulsey want to hurry away, back up to her apartment so nothing could make this conversation, this whole afternoon, less perfect. He wanted to see her again. He had said so. And she wasn't going to let that opportunity get by her. She was almost becoming accustomed to taking risks, and she set her sights on taking a chance with Warren.

FIVE

Several days later, when Warren found himself home early from work because of a power outage, he picked up the receipt with Tulsey's number on it and contemplated calling her. She was fun. They had a sufficient amount in common. Might be nice to have a friend so close, rather than having to drive forty minutes down to the city just to meet up with someone for a beer. She was a cute girl — not necessarily pretty, but cute — and she could have plenty of men. It's not like a call from me would make her swoon. She wouldn't assume I was necessarily looking for something romantic. After all, we're neighbors, and neighbors should hang out.

With that, he picked up his cell and dialed. She was there, and she accepted his invitation to come over for a beer. When she rang his doorbell a half hour later, he suddenly realized he had made a terrible error in judgment.

Tulsey was wearing jeans that hugged her hips, and a tight T-shirt that revealed nearly every inch of her modest chest. Her hair was curled. She wore dangling gold earrings and a matching bracelet, and she positively reeked of hairspray and drugstore perfume. Warren experienced a wave of panic. His heart raced and the back of his neck started to sweat. This was a mistake. She'd taken it all wrong. She'd gotten all gussied up to come over here for a beer. He had a brief flashback to his first night out with Linda, the woman he had unexpectedly broken up with on a lunch date at Gulliver's. Linda was prettier than Tulsey, and she had been a bit less obvious in her efforts to woo him, but it had happened exactly the same way. Warren had met her at a bookstore and had genuinely enjoyed her company. He took her number as a friend, but, before he knew it, the whole thing had slipped out of his control and he was in a relationship with her. Warren knew that explaining, or expressing himself, to women was not in his repertoire. He'd liked the company and the comfort of having Linda around, and it would probably be the same with Tulsey. But he could not be a true boyfriend. He had a reason, but the first time he said it aloud would not be in a pathetic attempt to ease a woman's broken heart.

He needed to get this under control as quickly as possible, in whatever way he could.

"So how was your day?"

It could have been innocent enough, but it sounded to Warren an awful lot like what a girlfriend would ask a boyfriend.

"Fine," Warren said. "Why don't you have a seat and I'll go get us a couple of beers."

"Sounds great," Tulsey said, taking the two steps down from the foyer into the living room.

When Warren returned from the kitchen, Tulsey had not sat down somewhere, as he had hoped. If she had, he would have been able to sit a safe distance away. Instead, she was gazing at the rows of books on his built-in shelf. She ran her finger down the spine of a couple, and then picked up a framed picture.

"Is this your family?" she asked.

"Yeah, that's all of us, about fifteen years ago," he said, handing her an opened bottle of Yuengling.

"Nice hair," she said, smiling up at him.

Her attempt to flirt by way of teasing annoyed him slightly, but he couldn't ignore the fact that her eyes were oozing some kind of electricity. They were a stunning dark blue, and they reminded him of the eyes an antique doll his mother kept in the living room breakfront of his childhood home.

"What can I say? I eventually had to let the 'fro go," he said, pulling his short curls through his fingers.

"Your hair is gorgeous," Tulsey said, setting down the picture.

Warren gave a half smile and took a gulp of his beer, then sat down at the far edge of the couch.

"I guess we've all got to grow up sometime. For me, it was letting go of my perm," she said, sitting down too close to him.

Warren could feel her energy. It was almost overwhelming. It was positive energy. Comforting energy. Completely unexpected, but it was the kind of energy that could lead to him giving something more than he wanted to give.

"I think I'm going to have another beer. Need another?" he asked, getting up and heading for the kitchen with his not-yet-empty bottle.

"I'll never turn that down," she said, draining hers.

When Warren came back, he handed Tulsey a bottle and sat in the chair next to the couch. He tapped his fingers on the worn knee of his jeans, and before the silence got awkward, he reached for the remote and clicked on the evening news. There was nothing sexy about news.

"Some quick thinking from a school bus driver and her students saves a pony from a pit bull attack. Find out how after this," the platinum talking head said just before the station broke for commercial.

Tulsey blew out a reverberating laugh that was so unbelievably uproarious, Warren couldn't help himself from laughing, too. He looked at Tulsey as she continued to carry on and saw that tears were dripping from her eyes. She held one finger under her nose as she leaned forward and back, forward and back, not trying to contain herself.

"Must be a slow news day," Warren said.

"At least they're reporting on something positive," Tulsey said when she was finally able to suck in a full breath.

"It's true," Warren said. He hadn't heard anyone laugh like that in months, maybe years. All of his friends and colleagues were too afraid of how they were being perceived to really let loose. He looked over at Tulsey, who was now fixated on a Doritos commercial, and felt a rush of appreciation. If the non-romance issue was cleared up without hurt feelings, he could see himself spending time with her. Relaxing into a friendship.

The news story didn't disappoint. Even the anchor was fighting back giggles as she read the teleprompter.

"Do you think that woman is proud of having to sit up there in front of however many thousands of people and relate a story like that?" Warren asked. "I wonder if she thought this is what she'd be doing when she got out of journalism school." He pointed one finger up in no particular direction and tilted his head to the side as Tulsey looked on. "Come to think of it, I suppose that's not that unusual."

"What's not that unusual?" Tulsey asked.

"Realizing when you get out of college that real life is nothing like the scenarios you were trained for. I mean, when I was in college and then graduate school, I had these visions of being part of some dynamic computer security team working to secure CIA data or something. I never imagined I'd be locked away in an office for ten hours a day, pecking away at a computer."

"Well, I—" Tulsey started before Warren interjected.

"It's like I'm a goddamned parakeet," he laughed. "Click, click, click, clicking away at my brick of birdseed."

"I never went to college. Just started working, so I haven't really been 'trained' for anything in particular. But I can tell you that my new project at work is to put thousands of checks into numerical order."

Warren said nothing and looked at her.

"I suppose it's more of a real job than what I had before I moved to Valiant."

"Oh, yeah? And what was that?" Warren looked over at the TV, which was now showing footage of a crane collapse. He picked up the remote and pressed the mute button.

"Worked at a deli. It's called Ronnie's. I was there for years."

Warren rubbed his thumb across his jaw line and over his chin.

"I'm surprised a girl as bright as you would settle for something like that," he said. As soon as he said it, he wondered if he shouldn't have, if he had somehow denigrated her work experience.

"The funny thing is, I never used to really think about it, you know? Most of the other kids I graduated high school with never went to college. They stuck around, started families young, and did whatever job they could get to pay the bills. None was better than the next, really. Of course, some kids stood to inherit some pretty big farms, so they didn't have to worry about what they'd eventually do to support a family. I guess I was thinking I'd just take over our small family farm when the time came."

"Must have been nice to know you always had something to fall back on."

"Yeah, I guess," Tulsey said, shrugging.

"But you went for something better," Warren said, looking at her. "You should be proud of that."

"Or maybe I just plain ran away."

"What's wrong with wanting a better life?" Warren asked.

"Nothing, I suppose," she took a deep breath, ran her hands through her bangs. "But I think I may have left for the wrong reasons."

"And what reasons are those?"

"My mom's got Alzheimer's. I couldn't stand the thought of sticking around and watching her disappear a little bit every day."

"I'm sorry," Warren said, getting up from his chair to sit next to her on the couch.

"Now that I'm here," she went on, "I don't feel any better. Worse, even. Guilty. I had great friends back there. I had everything I needed. I was always with my family. And for some reason it wasn't enough."

This wasn't the kind of thing Warren discussed when he went out for a drink with his buddies. It was all sports and money and girls and maybe a little bit of politics. He thought back now to the times he had sat with the men from his racquetball league and listened as they talked for hours about nothing. He would drift away into his own thoughts, wondering how it was that these men were all able to soldier on, getting up every day, putting on their suits, kissing their wives goodbye, kissing ass for ten hours and then, ultimately, collecting and depositing the check. Where was it, exactly, that everyone was trying to get to?

"Do you ever sit and think about where your life is going and come to the conclusion that it's really not going anywhere? Nowhere at all?" Warren asked after a moment.

"Says the man with the master's degree and the huge house," Tulsey said, waving her arm up to point out their surroundings.

"I've been doing the same thing for seven years. Seven years I have brushed my teeth in the morning, gone to work, and written computer programs. I interact with one person a day, on average. That would be the guy at the deli where I always get lunch. Tuna salad or turkey. Seven years," he said, nodding and staring absently at his blue Berber carpeting.

"This may sound ridiculous, but I always have some hobby to fall back on. Something to disappear into when I need to pretend my regular life isn't forging ahead."

"Oh, yeah? Like what kind of hobbies?"

"Well, first I painted, then I built kites. I learned how to do Origami, took up fishing, learned to ride a dirt bike. I even taught myself Spanish."

"Really?" Warren asked.

"For the last few years I've been really into woodworking. Had a friend who was into it and taught me a few things, then it sort of took off."

"No shit," Warren said, grateful to have an unexpected response. Her thoughts were honest, and she didn't pretend to have answers.

"Julie let me set up a workshop in her garage," she said. "Want to come over and have a look?"

Warren set his empty bottle down and stood up.

"Let's go," he said.

The two fluorescent lights instantly electrified the room and made the table saws, the sandpaper stacks, the toolboxes and the cans of varnish suddenly come alive from out of the darkness. Though the corners of the garage were caked with spider webs and clumps of long-ago dead leaves, Tulsey had made it look more comfortable by adding a small table lamp to the top of her work bench and a checkered seat cushion to the chair that Warren figured she must sit on when doing her work. There was a shelf holding a cigar box, a large carved wooden bowl, an intricate statue of a wizard whittled out of dark wood, and a birdhouse with gingerbread shingles affixed to the roof. There was a half-finished rocking chair next to the shelf, no doubt a larger and more involved project that Tulsey had been working on for some months. Warren inhaled a deep breath and welcomed the combined smell of wood shavings and turpentine, a smell that momentarily made him feel like he was not yet too old to have new experiences.

For that matter, he realized he was, at thirty-seven, not yet too old to be surprised by someone. This petite woman, this person who was trying to reinvent herself in the big bad suburbs, had created this workspace and everything in it with her tiny white hands and equal parts skill and will.

"How did you learn how to do all this?"

"Just sort of taught myself," Tulsey answered. "Went to a friend's house one day and saw that she'd made a chest of drawers from some kit she bought at the hardware store, and I thought I could do it, so I did."

She walked over to the rocking chair, which was upside down on the floor, and ran her hands over the unfinished wood of the rockers.

"Started out with little stuff, you know, boxes and things. Then I checked out some books at the library and learned methods for more advanced techniques, started working on a card table, then a picnic bench." She tucked her black hair behind her ear and walked over to the shelf. She picked up the carving of the wizard and handed it to Warren. He twisted in his hand, admiring the fabric folds carved into his robe.

"This little guy took me four months," she said, beaming.

"Exquisite."

"Carving is very different from building, but I love it all. The most amazing thing about woodworking is that I'm never thinking about anything but the task at hand when I'm doing it. It frees up my brain. Stops me from thinking so much."

She sat on the metal stool with the palms of her hands pressed down on the seat between her knees. Warren carefully placed the wizard back on the shelf and brushed away sawdust from the bench before he took a seat. He hunched over and put his elbows on his knees, then rested his chin in his hands. His thoughts started to wander, and apparently Tulsey's did, too, because she allowed the silence to continue for quite some time. This woman was doing what she wanted to do, what she needed to do to discover herself. Warren wondered why he couldn't bring himself to do the same. He always went the safe route. He had chosen a career that would pay the bills, a neighborhood that would be safe, and friends that had similar backgrounds. He had been raised to be conservative with money, time, and aspirations. It seemed like he hadn't tried anything new in months, maybe even years. He could hardly believe he was sitting in his new neighbor's makeshift woodworking studio rather than sitting at home on his computer, browsing eBay for newly released video games.

"What's it like to take care of Julie and Mark's kids?" he said, looking over at Tulsey. He didn't know why he'd asked. He'd simply wondered it in his head and it came out on his lips. No forethought, no adjustments to the way he asked it to try to control her perception, no self-doubt. Not that it was a controversial topic, but it was a new topic with a new person, which was a situation that would usually lead him to near excruciating levels of preparatory self-questioning.

"It's tiring, but every day I have them I can't wait to see their faces," Tulsey said. "I get to playing games with them and with chasing Lila around, and before I know it, the time is flying. They get annoying, and they cry and scream. When they get like that, nothing makes them behave better but a nap, and getting them to fall asleep requires some mystical power that I don't have."

Warren laughed. "Seems exhausting," he said.

"It is, but I much prefer it to the bullshit at the office."

Warren nodded, then sat up and wrung his hands.

"What's that?" he asked, pointing to a small stool that still only had two legs.

"I'm making a stepping stool for the kids. Lila's still too young, but Matthew needs it to get up to the sink. I'm tired of lifting him up to wash his hands. He needs to be able to take care of that and brush his teeth without me right there."

Her face went quiet, dreamy almost. She knew these children well in only a matter of months, Warren thought. She knew their routines, knew when they would behave and when they wouldn't, knew what they needed to work on to gain a little more independence. She must be falling in love with these children. There was no way around it.

"You want kids someday, don't you?" Warren asked.

Tulsey answered yes, but Warren didn't hear much of what she said after that. He had disappeared for a moment into his own thoughts as he imagined having children of his own to fill his house with laughter. He wondered what they would look like, but it hardly mattered except from a standpoint of pure curiosity. He could almost feel a future son's soft hair tickling his nose as he lifted him up so he could wash his hands at the sink. He could picture a relationship with his children, but he couldn't settle on an image for his future partner. Without that, or even with a clear image of a companion, he wasn't sure that raising children was in his future. The idea had always appealed to him, but he seemed to conceptualize it only in the obscuring haze of the distant future. He hadn't made any progress toward a family life. Up until this moment, in the garage with Tulsey, he hadn't thought about the fact that at thirty-seven, perhaps he was running out of time.

"Want to come upstairs for a drink?"

"Thanks, but I think I'm going to go for a drive. I need to zone out a little bit before I go to sleep. You know, recover from all this heavy thinking," Warren said.

Tulsey walked him to the end of the driveway.

"I had a great time. I'd love to do it again sometime."

"We didn't really *do* much of anything," Warren said.

"Still, I had a nice time."

"Me, too. I'll talk to you soon, Tulsey," Warren said. As he got into his BMW and closed the door, it occurred to him that spending time with Tulsey was the most self-serving thing he could do. He liked the attention. But after all of his regrets with how he handled his relationship with Linda, he could hardly believe that he had again lit up the same kind of dead-end fire in someone else.

Warren decided he needed a stiff drink. He rolled down the windows in his car, letting in the cool early fall breeze, and sped up Emerald Drive. He had once gone to a bar for happy hour just on the edge of downtown with that asshole from work, Lyndon Hoosier. It would still be open and would be the perfect place for him to sit in anonymity.

Warren wasn't much for speed, but on this late weekday evening, few people were on the roads, and he opened up on the highway and got a slight surge of joy from being able to take charge of something in his life. When he got off on the exit he usually took for work, he had to search within a couple of blocks of where he remembered Madigan's being, but he eventually found it, and much to his relief, there were only a few cars in the parking lot. He checked his watch. It was 10:30. Surely the place would be open until 11:00, if not midnight. He pulled into a spot and clicked his automatic lock when he got out, sending two beeps echoing between the surrounding office buildings.

The bar smelled of cigar smoke and was decorated with excessive amounts of brass and stained glass. The few lingering patrons sat alone or in twos in burgundy lounge chairs, nursing glasses of scotch or brandy. It was just the kind of old boys' club Warren was sure his obnoxious co-worker loved.

Warren heaved himself onto a barstool and was greeted by a weary-eyed woman whose loosened uniform tie hung with disinterest around her neck.

"What can I get you?"

"Rum and Coke."

She turned toward the shelves of liquor and Warren gazed around the room. Framed newspaper clippings of people shaking hands with presidents hung on the walls along with paintings of hunting horses and their riders. A large model airplane hung from the ceiling, nose slightly down to give the look that it was coming in for a landing between the bar and a row of booths. The room smelled of stale grill smoke and the floor, in need of the nightly vacuum, was scattered with flattened French fries and used sugar packets. There was a rather large group of diners in a separate party room, and Warren could hear their far-off laughter and see their shadows move in the dimmed light behind the frosted glass divider. The bartender placed a nearly clear rum and Coke down before him on the sticky bar.

"You look like you could use it," she said.

"Lemme get three chardonnays and a Jack and Coke." The voice came from over Warren's shoulder, and he turned slightly to see a thin waiter, leaning against the bar, holding a cork-bottomed plastic serving tray. He was tall and good-looking with light skin and light brown hair. He had appeared out of nowhere.

"That party's still goin' huh?" the bartender said to the waiter.

"Yup, and if I'm here this late, I might as well be making some money, so I'm happy to give them liquor all night," the waiter said, looking at Warren with a smile.

The bartender pulled a bottle of wine from the stainless steel refrigerator below the bar and uncorked it, pouring out three glasses that began to immediately collect condensation. She put together the Jack and Coke and placed all four glasses on the waiter's tray. He lifted it with ease and disappeared behind the divider.

Warren drew a long breath and leaned in to sample his drink. It burned going down, but after a few long sips, he felt relaxed and warm. He finished and ordered another. This one came just as strong as the first. A news magazine show was playing on the television above the bar. The set was muted, but Warren read the captions and watched as the pictures of a missing toddler from Ohio flashed over and over again on the screen while the narrator recounted the last hours before the little girl's disappearance.

Warren drained his glass and ordered a third. A while later, when he found himself barely able to continue reading the captions on the television, he wondered how many drinks he had ordered. He pushed his stool back from the bar and went to the bathroom on unsteady feet.

When he returned, the brown-haired waiter was sitting next to his stool, rolling silverware into cloth napkins.

"Mind if I do my side work here?"

Warren shook his head. He sat down and rubbed his fingers over his eyes.

"I'm Joey," the waiter said.

"Warren." He didn't outstretch his hand. Because of his fog brain he wasn't sure if it was the right decision, but for some reason, the gesture seemed too formal.

"Did you outlast your friends?" Joey asked.

"Nah," Warren shook his head, "I'm here by myself."

Joey smiled and reached for another fork. "Rough day?" he asked.

"I guess, though I'm not really sure why," Warren said.

"You don't need a reason to have a bad day. Some days are just shitty."

Warren was certain he'd never heard truer words spoken. He sat next to Joey, drinking ice water and talking about poker and the war. For the first time in some days he felt at ease and even safe.

When all the silverware was rolled, catsup bottles refilled and chairs lifted onto the tables, Joey flipped open his cell phone and called a cab for Warren.

"Don't worry about your car. We never call the towing company," Joey said.

"Thanks. I think I'll be taking a sick day tomorrow," Warren said, laughing a little too loud.

When the cab pulled up outside, Joey walked Warren outside. As he was stepping into the back seat, Joey handed him his number, penned in block letters below the Madigan's seal on a napkin. It was so easy, so surreal, Warren wondered if it was even happening.

When he got home, Warren placed the napkin down on his nightstand right next to his glasses, where he would be sure to see it when he woke up.

***

It was a freak October thunderstorm. The day had been warmer than usual; Tulsey watched the dark clouds move in over Valiant through the tinted windows of the bus on her way home from work. The lights on the bus flickered when it hit a pothole, and Tulsey gripped the purse on her lap. She welcomed the distraction of the storm, since she had spent most of her day at the office daydreaming about Warren. She had been so lost in thought that she had mixed up the numbered checks several times and had had to go back and find where she misfiled them. It had been several days since their date, which she wasn't really sure was a date, and she had not heard from him. She saw him once coming home from work, but he did not linger in his driveway or look over her way to see if he could catch up with her while she had a smoke at the top of her stairs. It seemed like he had a good time with her that night, but he did not make mention of seeing her again. This, she knew, was typically not a good sign. But Warren wasn't a typical man. He lived in a large house by himself, and he never brought women around. There was a seriousness to him that Tulsey had only ever seen before in people with secrets.

An old man dozed in the next row over, and two teenage boys bantered back and forth loudly about what kind of car could be outfitted with the best spoiler. Tulsey looked out both sides of the bus and then the front window to try and see where the storm was coming from. She'd been late to work that morning and hadn't had time to catch the weather report.

A bolt of lightning streaked through the sky, followed moments later by a billowing crack of thunder. The old man jerked awake. Large raindrops began to fall on the bus windows with loud pings.

By the time the bus pulled up to Tulsey's stop on Emerald Drive, it was pouring. The wind was ferocious. She took an abandoned *Inquirer* from one of the handicapped seats and held it over her head as she ran the quarter mile home in her heels. There was no way to avoid all of the puddles and rushing water, and eventually her shoes were soaked through, her pantyhose heavy with frigid water.

When she got to her apartment, she threw the saturated lump of paper down onto her porch and burst through the door. She ripped her dress while trying to pull it off and stuffed it in the garbage on her way to the kitchen to heat up the tea kettle. She traipsed over to her television in her bra and panties. When she flipped it on, her eyes immediately met a severe thunderstorm warning that scrolled across the top of the screen. Below, an out-of-breath weatherman pointed to a map of red blotches.

Tulsey walked to the window next to her door. The tall pines in the Curran's back yard swayed widely as chunks of hail began to pound the roof and windows. The tea kettle screamed from the kitchen, giving Tulsey a start. The television flickered off, along with the bathroom lights. The familiar hum of the refrigerator went silent.

Suddenly there she was with nothing to listen to but the rhythmic drops of rain on the rooftop. No commercials on television in the background, droning on about creams and pills and rubber band exercise systems. No sound of metal file drawers opening and closing amidst workplace chatter and the incessant ringing of the office telephone. No sound of old plastic seats rattling on the bus while cars below screeched around, their drivers perpetually honking in frustration. No sound of Lila and Matthew banging toys together. There wasn't even the whisper of another human being breathing in the same room with her.

How long had it been since she had nothing at all busying her ears but the distant rumblings of thunder?

Her eyes shifted in the fading purple twilight. She could see her mother's ragged fingernails, chipped and dirty from a day's worth of pulling weeds and scattering chicken feed, as she held up her cards, careful to conceal them from Tulsey's eyes in a game of Uno. They had played for what must have been three hours, getting through a series of fierce thunderstorms that pounded Lichten when Tulsey was a girl. The lights had gone out, and she had been so scared in the dark as the wind howled. Her father had told her not to worry, then sat on the couch and read a magazine. Her mother set up another flashlight on the coffee table and pulled out the deck of cards. Her mother's dark hair, not yet streaked with gray, was pulled back into a loose bun. Her soft young face broke into an overwhelming smile as Tulsey threw down one card and yelled "Uno."

Tulsey knew her mom never could stand for her to be upset. Much to the disappointment of her father, her mom had allowed her to sleep in her parents' bed until she was 18 months old. Tulsey had heard the stories many times. Her father had to finally put his foot down and take over the bed weaning process because Tulsey's mother couldn't be trusted to leave her alone in her crib to cry herself to sleep. The trend lasted straight through to high school, when her mom had taken her into the city to see a Gin Blossoms concert on prom night her junior year because Tulsey hadn't been asked by anyone.

Tulsey wondered if her mom had secretly been happy about her decision to move to the suburbs, if she was relieved to know that her daughter would not be around to watch her fall apart, one lost memory at a time. She imagined her mother being strong, forceful even, in demanding that her father not try to dissuade Tulsey from moving to a place where there would be more opportunity. She wondered if that conversation happened, and if it did, if her mother could see her father's face, licked by fear. He wouldn't – no, he couldn't be amenable to the idea of watching over his wife on his own. Everyone had limits, after all, and though Tulsey knew her father to be a strong man, she also knew him to be a sensitive one, likely to be bent and eventually crushed by the weight of utter helplessness.

Without realizing it, Tulsey had made her way outside her apartment and paused at the top of the stairs as the beating rain ushered in the darkness. Her mother's apple-red cheeks and the two petite, feminine moles at the base of her throat were all she could see. She opened the door and stepped into the cold rain, barely feeling the puddles collecting beneath her feet. The raindrops on her face were just a nuisance, small gnats that made her blink when they flew too close to her face. She leaned on the railing and looked out over Mr. Johnson's yard. She could pick out his twin trees, surrounded at the base by white granite rocks that picked up the last of the light and reflected it back like moons in orbit.

She listened as the gutters began to overflow and gush out onto the grass. Tulsey was there, alone in the dark, wearing only rain-drenched underwear. She had left her apartment door ajar behind her. She thought for a moment about being scared that someone – an ill-meaning stranger – might be lurking in the bushes at the end of the driveway, but her anxiety faded quickly, as if it, too ,were smothered by the darkness. She was a part of it. The rain, the blackness, the thunder, the wind. If she could stand out in these things with almost nothing on, she could become a part of anything. She could assimilate into whatever world she sought. She was at once an island, isolated from everything she knew, and a powerful wave, part of the grander tide as it crept up, inch by inch, on the mainland.

A flicker from one of the Dunboros' windows caught her attention. She blinked hard and wiped her eyes. She turned and saw the glow of flashlights, first one, then another and another from inside the house. She glanced left to Warren's place. He, too, had a flashlight moving behind his curtains. Moments later, Tulsey could see Julie's silhouette through the house window, illuminated by a candle.

She stood back from the railing and realized that she was shivering. She went back inside, toweled off, then pranced, naked and freezing, back to her dresser where she searched for a sweater and jeans. She struggled to pull clean underwear over her still-damp legs, and reached behind her back to clasp her bra. The sweater and jeans seemed to warm her, but she decided socks would be good, too. She fumbled through her bottom desk drawer and found her flashlight, which thankfully still had working batteries. She walked back to her dresser and held up the light as she searched through her drawer for her favorite fuzzy blue socks. She felt them and dug her hand deep into the pile of white and cream bras to retrieve them. As she did so, she realized she hadn't seen light moving around in Mr. Johnson's house. He might be in there, unable to find a flashlight. Or worse, he could have fallen on his way to get one.

Tulsey quickly pulled the socks on over her icy feet and stuffed them into her boots. She pulled on a raincoat, and set out for Mr. Johnson's place.

When she got next door, she paused for a moment and looked up at the shadowy wide pillars of Mr. Johnson's bungalow. The house was raised up a bit from the road, which Tulsey had never noticed until she was poised to walk up to the front door. It was a hulking structure, and she drew a breath and wondered if it wouldn't be better for her to turn around and head back to her place. Then she imagined the old man in there, sitting in his chair, struggling to lean over and pick up a pack of matches he had dropped while trying to light a candle with his shaky hands. She stepped onto the first flagstone step, made her way along the path and up the creaky wooden stairs.

She took the handle of the doorknocker and tapped it gently. There was no answer, so she lifted it up again and brought it back down on its metal frame with more force. After four knocks, she felt the handle coming loose. She withdrew her hand, and the doorknocker swung back and forth on the remaining nail connecting it to the door.

Slowly, the door opened. Mr. Johnson clicked on a flash light and held it up to Tulsey's face nearly blinding her. She raised her forearm over her eyes.

"Oh, sorry," Mr. Johnson said. He pulled the flashlight down and, in the indirect light, Tulsey could see he was standing with the aid of a walker.

The doorknocker continued to swing back and forth like a pendulum.

"Sorry about that," Tulsey said.

"Don't be. Damn thing's been broken for years."

"I'm Tulsey. I live next door. I met you at the Dunboros," she said.

"I know who you are." His voice was impossible to read.

"I didn't see any light coming from your place — not that I was looking in on you in a weird way or anything." She let out a nervous laugh. Mr. Johnson just looked at her. She cleared her throat. "Anyway, I just wanted to make sure you had a flashlight nearby – that you didn't lose it or drop it or something. But, obviously you have one, so I'll just head back to my place. Nice to meet you. Again." She turned on the porch.

"I was just about to start a fire," Mr. Johnson said. "Would you like to come in?"

"Oh, no, I should ... I have to go back home and— "

"And stare at the wall in the dark?"

Tulsey smirked.

"I don't want to intrude."

"It's not intruding if you're invited." He turned and pulled his walker around until he faced the opposite direction. The front door hung open between them. Tulsey looked inside tentatively, trying to make out the foyer in the dark. She could only see the silhouette of the stair railing. She followed the beams from Mr. Johnson's flashlight and pulled the front door closed behind her.

The house smelled like mothballs and must and the floor creaked. Tulsey could see a pile of freshly cut wood and a brass-handled fireplace tool set when Mr. Johnson rested his flashlight bulb-up on the floor. She stood and watched anxiously as he set aside his walker and lowered his hands toward the wood pile in slow motion.

"I can help you," she said.

"No, no. Have a seat. This is the only exercise I've gotten all day."

She tried not to look at him as he struggled to pick up one small log at a time and place it into the fireplace. Instead, she sat on the couch and attempted to discern what the rest of the room looked like in the dim light. She caught the edge of a cat as it made its way behind the couch, leaving only the end of its tall gray tail, held high and curved at the tip, in view. The furniture was old; it looked like it had been nice at one time, though now it was worn and punctured by cat claws. There was an abnormal number of clocks in the room; most were antique-looking and framed in carved woodwork. There were a few on the windowsill, another on the coffee table, and still two more atop the bookshelf in the corner. She could hear them all tick-ticking away at different intervals, filling the whole room with the reminder that no one was getting any younger.

"Do you collect clocks?"

"Only until I can fix them. Then I give them away," he answered. "The ones in this room I haven't fixed yet, so I keep them around to keep me busy."

Sooner than she had expected, a flame appeared in the fireplace. A crumpled piece of newspaper burned brightly at the base of a woodpile and the logs began to smoke.

"There we go," Mr. Johnson said. He turned and made his way into a La-Z-Boy chair across from where Tulsey was seated. He settled in and rested his intertwined fingers over his small belly. He leaned his head back slightly and made a sort of satisfied grunt, the way a dog does when he's comfortably bedded down for the night. He fell silent for a few minutes, and Tulsey bit her nails and pulled at her pony tail. She couldn't see his face all that well, and the lenses on his glasses were throwing around reflections of the fire, but she swore his eyes looked closed.

"Who's in the all the pictures on the mantle?" she asked, louder than she would have had she not suspected Mr. Johnson was napping.

"My wife and daughter, mostly," he answered. He turned his head to the side to look up at the photographs. "They both passed on from breast cancer two years apart."

"God, I'm so sorry," Tulsey said.

"It was a long time ago — almost twenty years now," he said. "Still miss them every day, but I got on with things, you know. Kept working and what not. Got easier after a while."

Tulsey nodded.

"So what brought you to Nacre Court?" he asked.

"Oh, I don't know. I was going nowhere. Working in a deli, still living with my parents. Plus, my mom is sick." She could hardly believe she said it, much less that she had said it to a man she hardly knew.

"Where did you move from?" he asked.

"Lichten."

"Lichten. Boy, I haven't been out that way in 40 years. Used to have a couple of cousins who worked in the steel mills. I'd go and visit them on weekends. It was a fun place to be — back then, anyway. Small town charm. Everybody knowing everybody else." He leaned forward in his chair and retrieved a wooden box from the built-in bookshelf next to his chair. "Mind if I smoke?" he asked.

Tulsey shook her head. He pulled out a pipe and packed it. He lit it with a match and pulled a drag, letting out a stream of smoke that moved slowly from his mouth up to his cheekbones and forehead and eventually up into the darkness of the room.

"What is your mother sick with?"

If it had been someone else asking her — someone she had just met that had not lost a wife and daughter to a slow and painful disease — she likely would have felt violated.

"Alzheimer's," she said.

"How long has she been sick?"

"I think about a year now. It had only been a few months before I left. I mean, she was increasingly forgetful, but we didn't have a diagnosis until this past spring."

"And how do you like it here?"

"It's pretty good." The answer came automatically. "Not great. I think I just need to get adjusted. Meet more people. I think maybe that's part of my problem." She paused for a moment. "I guess what I'm trying to say is it's not as great as I had imagined."

Mr. Johnson let out a deep, gravelly laugh. "Not for me, either."

Tulsey wasn't sure exactly what he meant. She presumed he was referring to his dead family, but she wondered if he might also be bothered by some of the same things that were starting to chip away at her confidence in her decision to leave Lichten. She couldn't escape the feeling that no one in Valiant was ever really listening to her when she spoke because they were either worrying about their to-do list or wishing they were talking to someone else. She hated feeling like she always had the cheapest clothes of anyone in her office. She couldn't stand the fact that Navajo Joe at the coffee shop was a white man. And Brenda Dunboro. Brenda Dunboro always made her feel like she was insufficient.

"There's nothing you can do for her," Mr. Johnson said.

"For who?"

"Your mother."

Tulsey wanted to tell him he couldn't be more wrong. She could make sure her mother saw all the best doctors and took the right medicines — they had drugs to slow down memory loss, didn't they? Tulsey thought she had seen a commercial for some such drug. She could make sure that she said all the right memory triggers around the house and that she did all the proper memory drills so her mom could retain as much as possible. And, when the time came that her mother couldn't live without professional care, Tulsey believed she could find the best place for her to live out the remainder of her days in as much peace and as little pain as possible. She had the intent to do this all along. Though she had moved, the responsibility had remained with her in some sort of marsupial-like pouch of her mind where she kept all of her deepest roles pressed against her, tight and warm.

She hated Mr. Johnson a little bit for saying there was nothing she could do. Yet she couldn't brush aside the notion that, having lost his entire family to breast cancer, he knew what it was like to have to let go and move on.

The lights flickered back on. Tulsey studied the room around her. The cherry bookshelves had been made by a skillful craftsman. The furniture was worn, but decorated with the same warm browns, oranges, and reds that were in the drapes. She turned and saw the kitchen, lit by an old Tiffany lamp hanging from the ceiling. There were newspaper and magazine clippings and pictures posted all over the refrigerator. On the floor next to where she sat was a giant stack of National Geographics. On a corner shelf, beneath a tarnished mirror, was a ratty teddy bear that still, all these years later, proudly held out a stuffed red heart that said "#1 Dad."

Mr. Johnson's home, now bathed in lamplight, was far less mysterious and menacing than it had been only a half hour before.

"Well," she said, "I'd better get home. I was going to try and do some laundry before work tomorrow."

Mr. Johnson began to stand.

"Oh, no, please. It's okay," Tulsey said.

Mr. Johnson disregarded her with a wave and took hold of his walker, following behind as she made her way to the door.

"It was a pleasure speaking with you. Thank you for inviting me in," she said, turning to him.

"The pleasure was mine," Mr. Johnson said, extending a soft, boney hand and giving hers a shake in the gentle and deliberate way that only a person of age can.

SIX

The great majority of the time, it wasn't possible for Julie to dwell on her decision to terminate her pregnancy. Her days were spent chasing the kids around the house, cleaning up their messes, making food for them, and persuading them to go to bed. When Tulsey was with the children, Julie was out translating for the school system to earn extra cash. She was certain that her friend Sue had meant well by offering to take Matthew and Lila to Disney on Ice with her family. The problem was that, once left alone with her own thoughts, Julie kept thinking of how or if she should tell her husband what she had done. She played out several of these imaginary conversations in her head, and every which way she dreamed it, Mark announced he was going to leave her.

She stood up and picked up the house phone to call Tulsey. Having her over for a drink would be a much-needed distraction.

Tulsey showed up a few minutes later, reeking of cigarette smoke. Julie poured her a glass of wine, and they sat down across from each other in the formal living room – the room they both spent a lot of energy trying to keep Matthew and Lila from entering. It was nice to sit with a friend in a civilized room without the constant clamoring of children.

"What time do the kids get back?" Tulsey asked. Tulsey was seated on the couch wearing a big sweater, jeans, and no socks.

"Sue said she'd have them back by 9:00. The show ends at 8:30, and it should take them a while to get back here from the city," Julie said.

Tulsey nodded absently and drank her wine.

"I think it's nice outside. Maybe I should open a window," Julie said. She walked across the area rug, feeling the awkward lump of the knot at the end of one of the rug's tassels under her foot. She unlatched one of the smaller side windows next to the bay window and tilted it open. She stuck her face to the screen and took a deep breath of the night air and its smell of wood smoke. She plopped back down into her green chair. "I can't believe how nice it is for the first week of November. Smells like somebody's having a fire. Don't know who would even want to have one – it's not that cold outside."

"Mr. Johnson," Tulsey said. "I think he builds a fire most nights."

"We should do something – get out of the house," Julie said.

Tulsey stood up and looked out the window toward Rick and Brenda's house.

"I've got an idea," she said, smiling.

Julie raised her eyebrows.

"Miss Brendie-Poo went to New York for the weekend to shop. She told me yesterday when I was out for a walk. She dumped the kid off at some friend's house because Rick has to work late tonight."

"And?" Julie asked.

"And so I think we should sneak into their hot tub."

"Are you insane?"

"Oh, for crying out loud, c'mon. What's the worst that could happen? Rick comes home and finds us in his hot tub?"

"Yes," Julie said shortly. Maybe calling Tulsey was a bad idea.

"Finding two women in his hot tub would be Rick Dunboro's wet dream. Besides, if those two clowns aren't going to enjoy what all their money has bought them, someone ought to on a night like this."

"Rick Dunboro is the HOA Nazi President from hell," Julie said. "He gets whatever he wants."

"What a powerful position," Tulsey said with heavy sarcasm. "I *bet* he gets whatever he wants."

"Well, he kind of does," Julie said, biting her lip.

Tulsey headed for the door, apparently on the way to change into her bathing suit.

It sounded like a bad idea to Julie, but it was still better than the alternative, which was sitting at home thinking about what she had done.

"All right," she said. "I'll get changed and meet you back down here in five."

Julie giggled when she went outside. Tulsey walked the stairs from her apartment clutching the bottle of wine they had opened earlier. She wore a blue robe with big white clouds sewn on like patches. Her flip flops were bright orange.

The brittle tree branches stood nearly naked against the star-filled sky, only a smattering of dead leaves clinging on by the sinews of their stubborn stems. There was a slight breeze, but it didn't yet contain full warning of the winter chill. Mr. Johnson's chimney patiently puffed a white stream of wood smoke into the air, filling the night with its tantalizing smell. The water in the pond rippled slightly, sending off sparks of moonlight.

Julie looked up and down the street sheepishly, as if she were readying herself to steal a candy bar from a drugstore. She was relieved to see that there was very little traffic up on Emerald Drive and that, for the most part, the street was dark except for a few dim lights coming from the upstairs of Warren's house. She watched in amazement as Tulsey walked across the street, just slightly in front of her, with an air of confidence bordering on entitlement. She carried the bottle of wine in one hand and a towel slung over her forearm. She held her chin a little bit higher than usual as she stepped onto the Dunboros' plush and leafless front lawn. Never once did she glance behind her in hesitation.

"Are you sure we can get away with this?" Julie asked, momentarily panicked.

"Yes." Tulsey stood on her tiptoes and looked into the Dunboros' garage. "No cars. We're all set."

They made their way to the back deck. Tulsey threw her robe over the banister and set down the bottle of wine. "Grab the other side," she said, pulling off the brown vinyl hot tub cover.

"You know, Rick has practically declared war against Mr. Johnson," Julie said.

"Mr. Johnson? Who could have a problem with him?"

"Rick could have a problem with anyone, but his latest target is Mr. Johnson. Says he doesn't keep up with his yard."

"Mr. Johnson's like eighty-something. Who gives a shit what his yard looks like? It's better than mine'll look when I'm his age," Tulsey said.

"Rick particularly hates the trees on the side of his yard."

"The magnolias?"

"I guess that's what they are. Anyway, Rick says they block his view of the pond."

"That algae-infested storm water management cesspool?" Tulsey asked.

Julie shrugged. "He says he should have a good view of the water – that not having one reduces his property value."

"What a dick," Tulsey said, shaking her head. "The last thing that asshole needs is more money. Let's piss in the hot tub on the way out."

"Gross," Julie whined.

Once the cover was off, steam rose in curls from the warm water. Tulsey jumped in the middle, throwing up a loud splash that sprayed all over the deck.

"Tulsey! That was so loud," Julie said in a forceful whisper.

She shrugged and began to fiddle with the controls. The jets began to bubble.

"We'd better not turn on the light," Julie said.

"All right," Tulsey said, "but the water needs to be warmer." She leaned her back up against the side of a jet, folded one arm over the side and took a swig from the wine bottle.

Julie settled into a seat in the corner. The bubbles worked on the muscles of her lower back, kneading their stiffness into submission. She let out an inaudible sigh.

"Mark loves hot tubs," she said. She hadn't spoken his name in quite some time, and it felt like a strange relief. "We talked about installing one of those bathtubs with jets in our bathroom, but then we got sidetracked with his deployment. We figured it was probably best not to spend the money right then."

"Probably wise," Tulsey said.

Tulsey handed Julie the bottle and she drank. She lifted her wrist out of the bubbles and pressed the button on her watch that lit up its green night light.

"Oh, shit!" she said. She squinted at the watch again. "Never mind. God, for a minute I thought it was already 9:00. It's only 8:00. I just looked at it wrong."

The two sat, indulgently taking in the warmth for several minutes before Julie spoke again.

"Do you … what's it like not to have to be anywhere for anybody?"

Tulsey gave a resigned laugh.

"No, I mean, really. What's it like to just be able to do what you want and not have to work in anyone else? You must just feel so free."

"Yeah, free except for when I have to be at work or help take care of Matthew and Lila," Tulsey said.

"But if you want to stay up really late one night because you're into some movie you're watching or something, you don't have to worry about getting up at 5:00 a.m. with your kids."

"Nope, I don't. Guess I never really thought about it that way."

Julie closed her eyes and laid her head back as Tulsey tried in vain to squirt water out through her clenched hands.

"And when you order pizza, what do you get on it?" Julie asked, suddenly sitting up again.

"Onions and green peppers. Sometimes just plain," answered Tulsey.

"I always order sausage because that's what Mark likes. I think sausage is repulsive, actually. The idea of all the leftover gristly pig parts being mashed together and repackaged as meat makes me queasy."

"So why do you eat it then?"

"I don't. I pick it off. But the pizza still tastes kind of like sausage."

Tulsey nodded and then suddenly took a huge breath, plugged her nose and dunked her head under the water. She surfaced a few seconds later, steam lifting off her face and shoulders and the water sizzling around her like popping soda bubbles.

"I think there's something about the warm water that makes you able to hold your breath longer," Tulsey said. "When I was a kid, my friends and I used to see how long we could hold our breath. I swear we used to get up close to two minutes."

"I don't think you're really supposed to put your head under water in a hot tub," Julie said. "Isn't it bad for you?"

Tulsey waved her hand dismissively and took a sip from the wine bottle. "How about you time me with your fancy watch?"

Julie shrugged and pressed the timer function, wondering if she had ever used it before now. The watch had been a gift from Mark.

"One ... two ... thr—" Her voice was cut off by the sound of her head plunging under.

Julie drummed her fingers on the side of the hot tub. Eleven seconds. She took a drink from the wine bottle. Twenty-one seconds. She looked around the backyard, squinting to see a birdhouse attached to a faraway tree. Thirty-two seconds. She leaned forward and looked up the road to see if, by any chance, there were headlights making their way onto Nacre Court. Darkness. Forty-six seconds. She peered into the dark water at the distorted shadow beneath the surface.

Tulsey surfaced, breathing heavy, and asked how she had done.

"Fifty-four seconds," Julie said.

"Good. Your turn," Tulsey said, reaching for Julie's wrist.

Julie protested, but Tulsey insisted. She unbuckled her watch and held it out.

"It feels good," Tulsey said. "Like you've just had a workout. You just become completely in to what's happening to your body."

Julie drew a deep breath and dipped under. She was enveloped by the muffled rumbling sound of the jets. The bubbles pushed at her from all sides and for the first time in weeks, maybe in months, she had nothing to focus on but the back of her eyelids. She could have considered how she was going to make the money stretch that month. She could have thought about getting to Jiffy Lube first thing in the morning on Saturday so she wouldn't have to wait in line so long. She could have thought about laundry or dry cleaning or scrubbing the toilets or shaving her legs. She could have even thought about Mark with a gun out in the middle of the desert. She could have worried about her children not recognizing their father when he returned. Worst of all, she could have feared that he would not return at all. But Tulsey was right. There were no thoughts. Just complete blankness. Not emptiness, just blankness where the only thing that could make its way through the wall and into her consciousness was how badly her lungs yearned for breath.

Julie sprung up out of the water. She sucked in air and wiped her nose.

"Forty-three seconds," Tulsey said. "Told you the warm water would make you able to hold it longer."

Julie said nothing and looked at Tulsey, feeling a rush of gratitude for making her do it. The only respite Julie got from the constant demands in her life was when she slept, and even then she was often haunted by her thoughts and fears, which would pull her awake and jab her again and again until, in spite of them, her physiology took over and demanded rest.

She watched as Tulsey tilted her head back into the water and floated, looking up at the sky. Maybe this woman — this stranger who had come into her life just months before as a result of an empty nanny position — had somehow come to understand her. Perhaps Tulsey, though she had no children of her own, could feel what it must have been like to have to give up your third child to God because your life was already so packed full that you had nothing left to give.

"We'd better get going," Julie said. "The kids will be home in a little while and I want to take a shower before they get back."

Tulsey got out and put her robe over her bathing suit. Julie dried off and put her sweat suit back on. They turned off the jets, placed the cover back over the water, and left only wet footprints on the Dunboros' back deck.

When they reached the front of their house, Tulsey walked with Julie to the front door.

"So, does the HOA get to decide what Mr. Johnson has to do?" Tulsey asked.

"Yep," Julie said. "They're discussing it at the monthly meeting tomorrow."

"You going?" She handed Julie the almost-empty bottle of wine.

"Seven o'clock. You wanna come?"

"I'll be there," Tulsey said. There was something in the way she said it. She could have had the tone of someone agreeing to go to a barbecue, or outlet shopping or to a cocktail party, but she didn't. Julie had invited Tulsey to come to a homeowners association meeting – which for some people would be only slightly more appealing than a trip to the dentist. Tulsey had intensity in her voice when she said she'd be there. And though the only light illuminating the porch was that from a single lamp glowing through two small windows at the top of the door, Julie could still see that there was fire in her expression. Yes, she would be there, not just at a meeting, but to witness for herself what the neighborhood bully would do. Rick Dunboro might be able to intimidate everyone else on Nacre Court, and in Gemstone Terrace for that matter, but Tulsey would not give him the control that others seemed not to even notice they were relinquishing.

***

Tulsey had only seen the upstairs of the clubhouse a couple of times. Mostly, she used the lower level where the locker rooms for the pool were. As she walked into the front door, Julie and the children by her side, she was reminded of how the clubhouse was itself a metaphor for Gemstone Terrace. The rug was a gaudy brown and cream swirled ordeal that would best fit Windsor Castle. The furniture was ornate but cheaply made, as evidenced by the one chair in the waiting room that was propped up with a dictionary in place of its missing leg.

The meeting room was more sterile, with gray carpet and dark maroon chairs set up in rows that faced the board table. Rick Dunboro was already seated in his chair in the middle of the table, behind the nameplate that read "President" that his wife had undoubtedly purchased for him. Brenda leaned over the refreshment table, her thin waist cinched by a black belt, and arranged cookies in rows on a platter. There was a bowl filled with fruit punch and topped with sherbet. When Brenda stood up and turned her face, Tulsey could see her inappropriately formal make-up, eyes lined in thick black and cheeks forced into a vibrant raspberry. Tulsey cringed. Did Brenda always wear that much make-up, or did she save it for special occasions?

Tulsey and Julie found seats at the end of a row so that if Matthew had to suddenly poop or Lila threw a tantrum, they would be ready. Julie sent Matthew to the back of the room to play Matchbox cars with Mattie Peterson. Julie bounced Lila on her right knee, patiently picking up the stuffed animal that she dropped every couple of minutes. People filed into the room still wearing their work clothes and looking haggard. An older blond woman sat down next to Rick at the board table, and they began to chat politely. Though she had been living in Gemstone Terrace for more than six months, Tulsey did not recognize most of the people who came through the meeting room door. A very large man in a green sweater came in, and behind him was Mr. Johnson. Mr. Johnson made his way to the far side of the room, patiently taking a step and then pushing his walker, which had two tennis balls on the legs. He wore a knit brown sweater that was pilling at the shoulders from wear, a pair of brown khaki pants that were too long for him, and scuffed brown boots. His metal-rimmed glasses had made their way down the bridge of his nose. He did not seem to notice anyone in the room. He sat by himself in the front row.

Rick cleared his throat. "The Gemstone Terrace Homeowners Association meeting is called to order," he said. The room went quiet. Rick shuffled some papers and spoke again. "The first item on the agenda is approval of last meeting's minutes."

The seven board members began to pore over the details of the minutes packet, correcting a few spellings here and there and arguing about some of the wording. Someone objected to the exact time listed that the clubhouse Christmas tree would be lit next month.

Lila gave a couple of stunted warning cries.

"She probably needs to be changed," Julie whispered. "I'll take her."

Tulsey stood up and took Lila from Julie's lap.

"I've got it," Tulsey said. She leaned over and grabbed the diaper bag.

"I'll bring Matthew with us and see if I can get him to go to the bathroom," Tulsey said.

She stood up and walked to the back of the room. Lila was starting to cry for real now.

"Matthew," Tulsey said, "we're going to go outside for a little while."

He grabbed his toy cars, stuffed them in his pocket and followed her into the lobby.

Tulsey reached into the diaper bag and pulled out a blanket, then spread it out on the lobby carpeting. She set the diaper bag down on a nearby chair and laid Lila out. She fussed at being put on her back, so Tulsey worked quickly to take off her overalls. Tulsey pulled off her dirty diaper and wiped her down, all the while speaking quietly to her, assuring her she could get back up in just a minute. Matthew whined about having to leave his friend behind in the meeting room, but then settled into playing with his Matchbox cars alone, running them along the metal railing of the wheelchair ramp as if it were a racetrack.

Tulsey dressed Lila again, and reached into the diaper bag to find her favorite stuffed animal. She also gave her an animal cracker from the small Tupperware container Julie had packed. She picked her up and, once she was quiet, walked over to the window and looked out on the cold, dark night. The last of the season's leaves swirled in the wind around the parking lot. Though a lot had happened, Tulsey still had trouble believing that it was almost December. Her time in Valiant seemed to have gone by in a haze of anticipation about Warren and in a constant struggle to find the motivation to go in to Shaw Marketing in the morning. At the same time, she could hardly believe where she was now in comparison to where she was at this time the previous year. Back then, she was still making biscuits and gravy all morning at Ronnie's Deli before switching over to chicken salad sandwiches in the early afternoon. It was Tuesday, and if she had still been back in Lichten, she surely would have had plans that night to go to Monica's house for the weekly poker game with the boys. She could see the bagful of empty Pabst Blue Ribbon cans that was always left on Monica's porch after game night, and she could taste the famous cheese dip that Monica always served with corn chips. The game was surely going on right now, some three hundred miles away, as Tulsey stood with a baby in her arms, looking out at the parking lot.

She felt a surge of anticipation at the thought of her planned trip home for Christmas. She yearned to talk to Monica and make things right again. Monica hadn't taken any of Tulsey's phone calls. Tulsey had left a few messages but quickly decided the only way her best friend would hear her out was face to face.

Tulsey also imagined walking into her parents' house for the first time in months. Her mother would be drinking coffee from a yellow mug while she sat at the kitchen table. Her father would be tinkering around out back or doing a crossword puzzle in the den. She realized that it had been some time since she had thought about her parents or let herself feel what it would be like to realize her mother was even more forgetful. It was more comfortable to just freeze them in her mind — her mother at the kitchen table drinking coffee, her father in his favorite chair in the den — than to think about how things might have changed for them since she'd been gone. She had spoken with them on the telephone a number of times, and they'd repeatedly told her that things were fine — great, even — but somehow she doubted it. They were probably protecting her.

It was what they would do. It was what they'd been doing her whole life. That was part of the reason she needed to get away.

Tulsey bounced Lila in her arms and walked over to Matthew to see if she could coax him into going to the bathroom. He flatly refused.

"Lila's all changed and she's calmed down now, so let's go back in and you can play with your friend," Tulsey said.

His response was something she could not have foreseen. He looked up at her and blinked a few times, then set down his cars and stood up from his kneel.

"Is it time for my daddy to come back?" he asked.

It reminded Tulsey of the time Monica's son had asked when his father, who had never been in the picture, was going to come find him. She hadn't known how to respond to Jonah back then, just as she had no idea what to say to Matthew now.

"Oh, Matthew," Tulsey said. She squatted down to look him in the eyes. His eyes were not Julie's at all, but his father's — big brown doe eyes, just like Mark's in the family photos at the house. She couldn't help but pass a hand over his head, ruffling his corn silk hair. "I don't think so," her throat got caught on the words. "Not yet," she said after a moment. "Did you ask your mom that question?"

"I asked her already." Matthew's eyes darted around the room.

"And what did she say?"

"She said Daddy was doing his best," he said.

"And did she tell you when he was coming back to see you?" Tulsey asked.

"She said in the springtime," Matthew said. "Is that a long way away?"

"Kind of," Tulsey said. She looked at the door into the board room, hoping that Julie would suddenly come through it, having had a sudden inclination to check on the kids. After a few moments, when Tulsey realized that a stroke of luck was not going to save her from having to really answer the question, she leaned over and kissed Matthew on the forehead. His head was warm and soft, like a newborn's, and he looked up at her, his eyes open wide with either confusion or anticipation or both.

"Actually, Matthew, the spring is a long time from now. It's not like a whole year or anything, but it will seem like a long time before it gets here."

Matthew nodded his head, then went back to running his red and blue toy cars over the railing. Tulsey was petrified that he would burst into tears, but she instead got no reaction at all. It was the same as if she had told him that he had a few more minutes to play and then dinner would be ready. There was no way he could understand time or what it would be like without his father for the next handful of months. But some day it would hit him that his father had missed much of his early childhood. First he would probably realize that he had no memories of him at his soccer games, and then he would think about the number of times he sat down to dinner with just his mom and his sister and then, finally, he would begin to wonder what it was that his father saw as so much more important than being with his son.

"Come on, Matthew, we're going to go back into the meeting. You can go play with your friend." Tulsey folded up the blanket she had changed Lila on and stuffed it into the diaper bag. She put the bag over her shoulder, readjusted Lila in her arm, and took Matthew's hand.

Tulsey quietly opened the door, and though she whispered to him to walk to the back, he took off running, which snagged the attention of a few of the attendees near the door. Tulsey could feel her face begin to flush, and she hurried back to her chair.

"Thanks for doing that," Julie said.

"No problem," Tulsey said, handing Lila and the teal teddy bear she was sucking on over to Julie.

Once Tulsey could again focus on the meeting, she realized the issue she had come for was on the table. Rick was speaking about the condition of Mr. Johnson's property. He listed all of the things wrong with it in agonizing detail: the splintering fence, the missing shutters, the ivy that had overtaken the side of the porch, the weeds that were growing in the side lawn, the length of the grass, the amount of time he left his trash and recycling bins out at the curb after pick-up, the porch light that had burned out years ago, the amount of time the leaves stayed on the ground before he had someone rake them up, the pinecones that littered his driveway, and on and on and on. Tulsey had noticed that Mr.

Johnson's home had a different look about it, but she had never thought it was because of neglect. It simply looked like an older home that had grown into the land a bit. Rick had apparently been keeping judicious notes about its condition for the last several years. As he spoke about it, his voice got louder, and Tulsey could see the muscles in his face tensing.

"I think we need to discuss issuing a series of citations for violations of HOA grounds keeping rules," Rick said. Though Mr. Johnson was in a seat just a few feet away, Rick spoke about him as though he were not there. At the same time, however, he avoided eye contact with him.

"After the last meeting, I did drive by Mr. Johnson's property a number of times to look at the condition, and it was invariably awful. In addition to the problems you listed, Rick, there is also a dead bush out front," said a tall, heavy man with a receding hairline.

"That's Bill Albertson," Julie whispered to Tulsey. "The biggest asshole in the neighborhood."

"I have issued Mr. Johnson several warning letters, but nothing has been done in response," Rick said.

Mr. Johnson raised his hand — a thin, papery shell over a mess of veins and knuckles.

"You are more than welcome, of course, to speak on your own behalf, Louis," Rick said.

Mr. Johnson stood slowly, steadying himself with his walker.

"As it turns out, that's why I came to the meeting tonight," Mr. Johnson said. Tulsey could detect the sarcasm in his voice, and she heard a couple of chortles coming from the back. It appeared that Mr. Johnson was not as in awe of Rick as most of his neighbors were.

"I have my property the way I like it." He coughed and phlegm gurgled at the base of his throat. He wiped his mouth with a white handkerchief.

Brenda winced and Tulsey caught it as she glanced around the room.

Mr. Johnson continued. "I have no desire to have it clipped and painted and trimmed. It's informal and so am I. I worked for fifty years to pay for my home, and I will do with it what I damn well please."

"There's no need to curse," Rick said.

Mr. Johnson swatted his hand in the air in disgust and took his seat. Rick raised his eyebrows and looked around the room, seemingly trying to gauge the response of the audience. The room was silent.

"I live next door to Mr. Johnson and I have no problem with the way his yard looks," Tulsey said without raising her hand or standing up.

"Miss Winslow," Rick's voice was crisp, determined, "with all due respect, you are not a homeowner in Gemstone Terrace. And while you are welcome to your opinion, it is not appropriate for you to express it in this venue."

Julie raised her hand. Rick nodded to her. She handed Lila to Tulsey and stood.

"I have no problem with his yard, either, for the record," Julie said.

"Duly noted, Miss Curran. Let's hear from some of the other neighbors."

"Mrs. Curran," Julie said before sitting down.

"What?" Rick asked.

"It's Mrs. Curran. Miss Curran is sitting on Tulsey's lap." Again, there were snickers from the back, but Rick continued, expressionless, calling on one neighbor after the other who named problems with Mr. Johnson's house. After all of the carrying on, Rick introduced a motion to issue three one hundred dollar citations to Mr. Johnson: one for his chipping paint, one for his missing shutters, and a third for his weeds. The board voted in favor, with no one opposing.

Mr. Johnson sat silently.

"The biggest issue of all, as far as I'm concerned," Rick said after the vote, "is the state of the trees on the edge of his property. As I mentioned in the last meeting, not only are they terribly overgrown, but they also block my view of the golf course pond, and in doing so reduce the value of my property. At the next meeting, I propose we discuss requiring him to cut them down."

"Are those even technically on Mr. Johnson's property?" The blond board member chimed in.

"I've done the research, and though the trees are right on the edge of his property, it is technically still his property and not golf course land," Rick said.

With no other items on the agenda, Rick declared the meeting adjourned, and Tulsey and Julie gathered the kids and got up. When they got to the lobby, Matthew announced that he needed to pee, so Julie took him into the bathroom and Tulsey waited with Lila. Most of the people who had been at the meeting filed past her, avoiding eye contact. Mr. Johnson came lumbering by and nodded his head.

"Thank you, Miss Tulsey," he said. "Good night."

"Good night," she answered.

Matthew came bounding out of the men's bathroom, and Julie helped him get on his jacket while Tulsey pulled Lila's from the diaper bag and put it on her. As they walked to the minivan, Tulsey turned to look back at Mr. Johnson. She saw him there, in the shadows, making his way to his car with his walker with all the patience and deliberateness of a chess master contemplating his next move.

SEVEN

"Mom?" Brenda Dunboro heard her daughter, Laura, ask.

"Yes, sweetie?" Brenda answered. She gripped the steering wheel and guided their SUV into the Westland Elementary School parking lot.

"What if I don't do good?"

"Well, you mean," Brenda said, looking over at her daughter in the passenger's seat. "What if you don't do well. You'll do great. You've practiced and practiced. You know all the steps – you showed me last night."

"I know, but sometimes when I get up in front of people I get nervous and I can't remember," Laura said.

"You'll be fine, honey. Perfect, I bet," Brenda said, smiling at her daughter.

Brenda slid the car into park and flipped down her sun visor to check her face in the mirror. She touched up her lipstick with the tube she kept in the console and ran her finger over her teeth to make sure no color was spotting them. Laura hopped out of the car, ballet bag in hand, and took off for the gymnasium door.

"Where are all the girls getting ready, Laura?" Brenda shouted to her daughter, who was already a ways ahead of her. "In one of the classrooms?"

"No, in the girls' locker room," Laura said before she pushed open the door and disappeared inside.

"I'll meet you there," Brenda said, knowing her daughter hadn't heard her. She gathered her purse, the tote with Laura's stage make-up, a bag of pretzels and a packet of carrot sticks that she had brought along in case Laura got hungry before the show. The parking lot was still vacant except for a shiny red minivan that still had its interior lights on and an old clunky blue sedan that dipped so low it nearly touched the gray, pebbled pavement. Brenda buttoned her heavy fleece jacket and made her way inside.

Two men dressed in janitor uniforms were meticulously placing chairs in rows inside the gymnasium. One of the younger ballet teachers was arguing with her husband on stage as they tried to straighten the hanging canvas painting of a regal staircase that was to be the set backdrop. It was tilted at a 45-degree angle and the teacher was frantically reaching to balance it when Brenda walked past and into the hallway.

Only one other dancer — a girl who was also playing a mouse — and her mother had arrived when Brenda walked into the dank locker room.

"Over here, mom," Laura called.

"You should drink some water," Brenda said. She handed her a water bottle from her purse. "Your costume is going to be very hot under all the stage lights."

Laura twisted open the bottle of water and took a long, eager drink.

"I brought snacks in case you get hungry."

"Thanks," Laura said, handing the half-empty water bottle back to Brenda.

Other dancers and their mothers trickled into the locker room. An hour later, Laura was dressed in a fuzzy brown leotard, her face painted pink and dotted with fake whiskers.

"You look so good!" Brenda exclaimed when her work was done. "Just like a little mouse!"

Laura looked at herself in the mirror and giggled, putting a hand up to her face.

"You can't touch your face, honey!"

Laura looked at the palm of her hand, where there was a large brown and pink smear of make-up. Brenda took two paper towels from the silver box mounted next to the sink and pressed and wiped hard at Laura's hand.

"You just need a little touch up," Brenda said, pulling a stick of make-up from out of the tote bag. She dabbed it on Laura's nose and around her lips. "Okay, let's go find Miss Ellie."

Miss Ellie was backstage lining up all of the dancers who were to perform in the opening scene. She patiently guided the youngest dancers into line with a careful hand on the back of their shoulders. She continuously looked over her should to make sure they had not strayed.

"Just do what Miss Ellie tells you." Brenda kneeled to look her daughter in the eyes.

Laura nodded and looked around anxiously at the commotion back stage.

"I have to go sit in the audience now. Good luck!" Brenda gave a small wave and walked away.

She sat in one of the folding metal chairs next to an elderly woman who smelled like talcum powder and was peering at the stage through the top of her thick bifocals. Brenda draped her sweater over the back of the chair next to her and put her purse on the seat so there would be no mistaking that it was reserved.

Parents, grandparents, young friends and extended relatives piled into the gymnasium. They filled up row after row and then more stood against the walls. Men wore khaki pants and sweaters or button-down shirts. Women wore dress pants or skirts, while teenage siblings forced into attendance wore jeans.

"Excuse me, ma'am? Is this seat taken?" a smartly dressed older gentleman asked Brenda, slightly leaning into the row and pointing at the seat next to her.

"Oh, yes," she said. "My husband is coming."

"All right," the man said before he disappeared back into the crowd.

As everyone settled and lowered their voices to whispers, Brenda checked her cell phone to see if she had missed any calls. When she saw that she had no messages, she stood halfway up and looked around the room just as the lights were going off to see if Rick was standing by one of the doors and searching the crowd for her. There was no sign of him, so she smoothed the back of her skirt with her hands and sat. Plenty of other fathers had managed to be there on time, she thought. He had so many excuses for being late. These days it was like he had a bag of explanations from which he drew when he needed to keep her questioning at bay. Surely not everything he had to do was more important than his family.

Before the lights came up on stage, the music started far too loudly and was quickly turned off. On the second try, the sound of a recorded piano punching out a dramatic tune came on. The curtain lifted on Cinderella, played by a beautiful young girl with an ugly blond wig. She scrubbed the floor in her evil stepmother's foyer. The girl stood up and did a sad dance to the music, inserting a swipe with a feather duster every now and again. After she finished, a boy came out to the podium and stood beneath a spotlight to recite a summary of the first part of the fairytale.

Three scenes later, Brenda could see all the little mouse dancers lining up in the shadows just off stage. She nervously looked around the room once more for Rick, but he was nowhere to be found. She straightened herself in her seat, pulled her camera from her purse, and lifted her head to get a clearer view of the stage.

One by one, the little mice twirled their way onto stage and began to dance in a circle around Cinderella. The last was a little boy who came dangerously close to tripping over his own foot with each labored rotation. Laura leaned over and picked up the end of Cinderella's dress and shook her finger in shame at the fraying, dirty hem. Cinderella danced her way off stage and the mice lined up. A person offstage handed them sewing props – a couple of huge pairs of purple foam scissors, a big thimble made out of aluminum foil, a giant Styrofoam spool of yarn – that they passed one by one down the line. The mice danced around briefly before one of the older dancers went off stage and returned running daintily, holding a huge piece of fabric that flowed in waves behind her as she held one end above her head. The lights went down.

The gym lights came on a moment later for intermission, and Julie stood up and clapped loudly along with the rest of the cheering crowd. As the applause died down, Brenda grabbed her purse and sidestepped her way out of the row and left the auditorium. In the hallway, a young girl and her mother manned the PTA fundraising table. They sold cookies, brownies, coffee and soda, collecting money and doling out change from a rusting metal box. Brenda reached in her purse and pulled out a five-dollar bill.

"I'd like a Diet Coke," she said, handing money to the young girl. As she started to make change, Brenda interrupted. "Keep the change," she said.

"Thank you," the girl said shyly.

Brenda tapped on the soda can before she opened it, then walked around the corner to where several other parents were standing. The drink was cold and super sweet and eased the tension in her temples ever so slightly. She took small, polite sips, and stared out the window at the courtyard below. The abrasive orange glow of fluorescent lights lit up the twiggy trees, picnic tables, and patchy brown grass below. Inside, the hallway hummed with pleasantries. Brenda turned and went into the bathroom. She looked in the mirror. Her hair was a disaster and her lips were a pale, sickly pink. She couldn't bring herself to care. She dumped the rest of her drink down the drain and threw the can in the garbage.

As she was heading out of the bathroom, swinging her purse over her shoulder, she saw another dancer's mother, whom she knew only as Roberta. Roberta was overweight, loud, intrusive, and way too friendly. She lived in Arter Woods, the poorest neighborhood in Valiant.

"Well, hello!" Roberta bellowed.

"Nice to see you, Roberta," Brenda said, looking for an opportunity to make this just a passing hello. Roberta forced the issue.

"How are you?" Roberta asked, stepping closer, bringing with her the stench of cheap perfume.

Roberta had begun talking to Brenda one evening while the two waited in the lobby of the ballet studio for their daughters to finish class. Roberta's daughter, Lexa, was much older than Laura and was a marginally proficient ballet dancer.

"I saw Lexa as the evil stepsister — she looks great," Brenda said politely. "What an excellent costume."

"Oh, you know, she just loves it. Absolutely loves ballet. She's never really gotten into any other activity. They just haven't interested her, you know?"

Brenda nodded.

"She's hoping to be a professional dancer one day — not necessarily a ballet dancer — but I'm just glad she's getting the exercise."

She sure needs the exercise, Brenda thought. Lexa's leotards always squeezed her plump body, looking as though a seam might burst at any moment. It was clear that Lexa had inherited her mother's slow metabolism. Not only was Roberta large, but she accented it by always wearing loud floral print shirts and dresses with matching headbands. Today was no exception. Her dress was a dusty dark blue with a pattern of bright roses and kissing white birds. Her feet were shoved into worn black pumps, and her fat ankles bulged in spite of her tight pantyhose.

"Laura really likes ballet, too, but to tell you the truth, she likes horseback riding the best. She takes lessons at the Valiant Equestrian Club. We are thinking about buying her a horse."

"How wonderful!" Roberta exclaimed, as if she understood what it felt like to be able to pay for a horse.

"She also plays softball and field hockey in season," Brenda continued.

A little girl, dressed in a blue tutu, walked through the crowd ringing a small silver bell.

"I guess it's back to the show," Roberta said. "It was great to see you, Brenda. I'm sure I'll run into you soon at the ballet studio."

"Take care, Roberta," Brenda said, relieved.

Brenda strode quickly to the exit and popped her head out, looking around the parking lot for Rick's car. She didn't see it and no one was outside. He was officially going to miss the entire show. What an insensitive bastard he was. A blustery wind blew at her face, and she struggled to pull the door closed. She hurried back to her seat and sat down just as the dancers for the second act were coming onto the stage. Though Laura only had a small part in the second half, Brenda found herself engrossed in the performance. As the dancers playing Cinderella and the Prince made their way around the stage during the ballroom scene, Brenda remarked at the tenderness they both had in their steps; they moved together as though they were one inseparable force, feeling each other's heartbeats. How young they were, Brenda thought, to have such an intuitive understanding of intimacy.

When the curtain dropped on the final scene, Brenda sprang up, clapping vigorously along with the rest of the crowd. The dancers filed on stage to take their bows, and Laura took a collective bow with the other mice.

"Yay, Laura!" Brenda yelled.

As the crowd disbursed, Brenda made her way to the locker room to look for Laura. Just as she reached for the door, she felt a hand on her arm. She knew it was Rick before she turned around.

"I'm sorry, honey. How'd she do?" He looked over his shoulder as he asked. His mind was still someplace else.

"Fine," Brenda said evenly. "She was great, actually."

"I knew she would be," he said. "How about I take the two of you out for dinner?"

"We had dinner hours ago. If she doesn't eat before her shows, she gets a headache."

"How about dessert, then?"

Brenda didn't respond, but instead reached for the locker room door. She left Rick behind and found Laura inside. Laura was with some friends in the corner by the showers.

"Laura, good job, sweetie!" Brenda squealed as she made her way over. She reached her arms out just the tiniest bit before she realized that her daughter might be embarrassed by a hug. "We should get your stuff and go — Daddy wants to take us out for ice cream."

"He made it in time?" Laura asked.

Brenda took a deep breath. "He thought you were wonderful," she said.

"I have to go, guys — see you at school," Laura said to her friends.

Rick gave Laura a big hug and rubbed his hand over the top of her head when she came out into the hallway with her mom. He looked questioningly, and Brenda knew he was asking if she had told their daughter the truth. She shook her head.

"You were wonderful, Laura," Rick said.

"Thanks, Daddy."

Later that night when Laura was asleep in her room upstairs, Brenda sat on the family room couch staring blankly at the television, flipping through the channels. Rick was in the kitchen making peanut butter toast, which he would probably drizzle with honey. She could hear him pouring himself a glass of something — most likely orange juice, which he only drank at night. He walked into the family room, toast and orange juice in hand.

"Thanks for covering for me," he said as he sat down. Brenda pretended to be intently watching a cooking show in which the chef was preparing chicken soup from scratch.

"The secret is to boil the chicken's feet in the broth," the chef said excitedly. "It gives the flavor fullness that I haven't been able to find any other way."

Rick looked at the television, looked over at Brenda, then bit into his toast.

"Don't ever ask me to do that again," Brenda said, still looking squarely at the TV screen.

"You know I do this for you," Rick said. Though it was in a near whisper, he forced the words out of his mouth the way a geyser blows steam before it bursts into a spout. The tendons in his neck were strained. He uncrossed his legs and put his foot down on the floor. He leaned in, grabbing the lace-edged sleeve of Brenda's nightgown and twisting it in his fist. "Do you think I would work like this if I didn't have to?" Tiny droplets of his spit landed on her cheek. He threw her arm to the side as though he were throwing away a dirty napkin and calmly walked upstairs.

Brenda sat still for a moment. The vision of the rail-thin domestic diva on the television screen blurred as her eyes filled thick with tears. She looked down at her arm and rubbed it to make the stinging go away. She pulled up the satin and inspected her forearm. He had not left so much as a red mark.

The next morning, after seeing Laura off to a friend's house, Brenda sat at the kitchen table, both hands wrapped around a steaming cup of coffee. She was hunched over, staring at the wisps of vapor as they rose up into the sunlight when her husband peered at her through the living room. He wore crisp khaki pants and a button-down, covered by a blue argyle sweater vest.

"It's quite warm out today — an Indian Summer," he said as he retrieved his keys and wallet from the table by the front door. "High is supposed to be almost sixty. I'm meeting some of the guys at the club to play eighteen."

"Okay," Brenda said weakly.

"See you later, then," Rick said, and the door closed swiftly behind him.

Brenda drummed her fingers on the kitchen table and thought about what she had to do that day: go to the drycleaners, drop off the clothes at Goodwill that Laura had outgrown, call her mother, email her friend Betsy a cookie recipe. She usually read the paper in the morning, but it remained in its plastic bag at the end of the driveway.

She thought about going out somewhere just to get out of the house, but nowhere sounded good. The other two stay-at-home mothers she knew were total bores. Their afternoons together always started off with an exchange of the latest trials in their lives: the phone bill was wrong, the PTA meeting ran late, the husband let the kids eat microwave popcorn for dinner. Then, it was onto a kind of competition about who handled their tribulations the best. And there was a lot of talk about weight, exercise, and how much they had resisted or splurged that week.

Cup after cup of black coffee later — no creamers or sweeteners; they added hundreds of calories — Brenda finally settled on taking a nap. She went upstairs, pulled down the shades, got into the unmade bed and closed her eyes. Thoughts kept coming to her in the darkness — slowly at first, then with increasing speed.

She could see Rick's face and feel the way she used to yearn to smell him after he had shaved. She could see herself before she met him. She lived in a dingy apartment way across town, sitting alone against the bare walls at night, alone with the television, blinking slowly as her life passed. It had been so hard that one year she had been out on her own. Everything had made so much sense when she met Rick. Marrying him was natural, their future together clear and enticing. She sat up, pulled her knees to her chest and rubbed her legs, the legs that had not been smoothed by touch in months. Even when she and Rick had sex, they barely touched at all now. Instead, it was methodical and efficient.

She imagined what her parents would say if she told them she planned to divorce the man they had so badly wanted as an addition to the family. "Rick is a good man, and a great catch," her mother had told her. She imagined the helpless, sympathetic whines of her friends as she told them that it was over, that the end of the line had come much, much sooner than expected with her marriage. That indeed it would not be death that parted them.

Brenda had never allowed herself to think about what would happen afterward if her domestic life came to some spectacular, fiery finale. She had talked herself so well into believing that this was different, that the struggles she had had in relationships past were over now. Rick was her man. He was the one. There would be no falling out the way there had been with the other men — boys, really.

The thought of starting over again, without a house to manage and food to make and parties to throw and attend, was too massive for Brenda to absorb. With little work experience, how would she make a living? Would her only option be to work as a domestic employee, doing other people's dirty laundry and scraping their dishes and wiping their babies' asses the way all the Mexicans did? What if the only job she could get was as a maid for another woman in Gemstone Terrace? Oh, God, she thought, with trembling hands. Her chest started heaving, and it seemed harder and harder to catch a breath. She looked around the room frantically for something — a DVD, a bottle of nail polish — anything that would occupy her hands long enough to let her mind slow down.

Her darting eyes landed on the laptop, half-buried by the pajama pants Rick had pulled off earlier that morning. She sat on the floor and flipped it open with the anticipation of a treasure hunter throwing open a long-sought-after treasure chest just exhumed from the murky and treacherous depths of the Pacific. She clicked on the Internet Explorer icon, and went to the Google page. In the search box, she typed one word. It was the only word that could become the saving force for her marriage and her sanity. It was the embodiment of what she needed now and what she had always needed. It was a word with many meanings, many fulfillments.

With quivering hands, she spelled out "companion" and then clicked "Enter."

***

In a brave moment brought on by near unspeakable boredom from organizing canceled checks, Tulsey had emailed Warren from her desk at

Shaw Marketing with the request to join her in an eight-week woodworking course at Valiant Community College. She had included the link to the Web page with all the details, including the price of $168. Tulsey really didn't have $168 to spend on a woodworking class that was well below her skill level, but she hadn't heard from Warren in weeks and she was desperate to see him. A woodworking class would mean repeated exposure, and inviting him was not like asking him out on a date. Besides that, Tulsey couldn't help but notice that he never seemed to leave his house, and that his lights were going out earlier and earlier each night. Much to her surprise, he emailed back with one word: "Sure."

Warren would drive them both to the woodworking studio, where they sat down with five other people, all of whom looked to be at least seventy-five years old and who had apparently been referred to the class by the Seven Heights Senior Center.

The teacher, Mr. Roy Robinson, had a thick silver beard and glasses, and unapologetically wore the same brown sweater for every class. He was also a set designer at Valiant Community College and spoke of their productions as though they were Broadway masterpieces. He was pretty attentive as a teacher, if for no other reason than the liability inherent with saws.

Mr. Robinson began each weekly class with a fifteen-minute tirade about how the world had once again seized him and pumped him full of the venom of ghastly misfortune. One week it was about his physical ailments: psoriasis, acid reflux and migraines. One week it was about the unappreciative administration at the Community College, which he said had not taken notice of the sets he and his students had built this year, although they were just as fantastic as in previous years despite a budget that had been slashed in half.

At the last class before the holiday break, Mr. Robinson chose to tee off against his twenty-three-year-old son, Geoffrey. Geoffrey was working as a stockbroker. According to Mr. Robinson, he was "pretentious, ungrateful, and wormy." He stopped short of calling him an actual worm, instead settling for the slightly safer adjective form of the word.

"It seems this new generation coming up has a real fascination with their titles and their dollar amounts, and my son is no exception," Mr. Robinson said.

June, a classmate who had been thoroughly sanding a cigar box she had made, looked up at Mr. Robinson for the first time that night. Tulsey found his rant endlessly entertaining and listened intently, though she looked away every time he tried to make eye contact, for fear he might somehow find a way to aim his anger at her.

"When I was coming up, if you put a roof over your family's head and food on the table, you were a success. You were an honorable man," he declared. "But these days, sheesh," he emphasized his disgust with a disbelieving half-shake of his head. "I'll tell you what, if you don't pick your life's path by the time you're ten years old, you've missed the boat – banished to the underworld of mediocrity," he said. "My son informed me last weekend that I was 'a card-carrying member of The Underachievers Society.' He told me that after I gave him a hard time for not having come to visit me and his mother for four months. And you know where he lives? He lives three miles away." His face was turning red now. "Never mind that I sent him to the fancy college where he got his 'education.' Seems they left a few things out of the curriculum."

When he finished, the class was, per usual, looking around awkwardly, waiting for him to switch gears and finally start taking about the malleability of shagbark hickory again.

"I've heard being a stockbroker is the second most stressful job there is, just after being a doctor," Tulsey said.

"Hmmm," Mr. Robinson said with exaggerated skepticism.

"I have to presume that stress like that makes people act like assholes," she said, wondering afterward if she should have toned down her language for the older set.

Burney, the most outspoken senior in the group, snickered from his workstation.

"All right, let's get started," Mr. Robinson said after a strange silence.

As he carried on about the intricacies of steam bending wooden rods, Tulsey stared at Warren, watching him as he tried to pay attention to the lecture. He would often drift off, staring out the classroom door or at the corner with the large filing cabinet topped by ferns. His face held a combination of intense anxiety and apathy. His eyes were shallow and steely, his forehead perpetually wrinkled with displeasure. Tulsey watched him that night, as she had watched him during all of their evening classes, as he pushed himself to focus – pushed himself to listen, to sand, to cut, to saw even though he accomplished tasks much slower than the rest of the class. He had not yet made a top for his cigar box, and the small model airplane that was his first project lay without wings on his workbench. Still, Tulsey reasoned, the class was getting him out of the house. Perhaps he took it on because he knew that he needed something to fill his time, even if it was something mundane and something for which he held little interest.

She tried to look away and focus on her own work, telling herself that Warren was an adult and could handle his own affairs. But her gaze kept gravitating toward him and zeroing in on his obvious pain until, only an hour into the two-hour class, she walked over to his work bench, sat on a stool and looked him straight in his forlorn eyes.

"Do you wanna get out of here?" she asked.

"Please," he said, with obvious relief.

They packed up their bags and told the class she wasn't feeling well. Warren had driven her, she explained.

They opened the door into the frigid air, and before they had gotten down the stairs, Warren flung off his backpack and let himself fall heavily onto the cement, his rear barely getting under him in time for him to take a seat. Tulsey stopped dead. Warren put his face into his arms and exuded silence that was, after an excruciating anticipatory pause, punctuated by the sounds of heavy sobbing. Tulsey sat quietly beside him.

She could not guess what was troubling him, but she doubted it was anything sudden. If there had been a death in his family, she was sure she would have heard of it. Same thing if he had been laid off or mugged or wrongly accused of a horrible crime. She was relatively certain that the issue getting him was much slower burning. She had not yet known him a year, but she could tell that he was in a different place than he had been when she moved to Gemstone Terrace. He was deflated. The joy was gone from his voice. The interest and wonder he had displayed were buried somewhere.

She was torn about whether or not to touch him. Some people needed space. She looked around the parking lot and was glad that all of the students were either still in class or gone for the evening. Her friend had a critical need for privacy, and Tulsey, in a strange sort of way, felt humbled by the fact that she happened to be at his side. She looked at him for several seconds as he shook, crying silently but so hard he had to struggle to catch a breath. She reached over and rubbed his back through the softness of his down jacket.

"I'm sorry," she said, drawing her hand back. "Some people don't like to be touched when they're upset."

"No, it's okay," Warren said, looking up at her for the first time. His eyes were red and his face had a deep look of confusion. A dribble of snot peeked out from the base of his nostril. He wiped it away on his sleeve as he looked at her.

It was bitter cold, and their breathing gave off alternating puffs of white mist. Tulsey was nearly frozen, but she sat still. Warren was having his moment, and that was more important than her discomfort. If they were to get in the car and drive home to have a warmer place to do this, it would be at his suggestion, not hers.

Warren gave his face a deep, heavy rub and then looked at her, speaking forcefully.

"Why does it look so easy for everyone else?" he asked.

"What? What looks easy?" Tulsey asked.

"Living," he said flatly. "Why does it seem like everyone else is just coasting along, and I have to grind through every single day? Every... single ... day," he repeated, not seemingly for emphasis, but rather so he could get his own mind around the enormous task of existence.

"Is it your family?"

Warren didn't answer.

"Work?" she asked.

"All of it," he said. "Everything. Staring at a computer screen all day, pretending the people I work with wouldn't screw me in a half-second if it meant so much as a free meal for them, my stuck-in-the-fifties parents, my brother and his perfect fucking family. He has twins. My younger brother has twins. And my parents look at me like I'm half a man. Like all I'll ever be is a career man. Never a family man." He sucked in air through his teeth and went on, "And fucking Gemstone Terrace. I hate Gemstone Terrace. I've hated it since the day I moved in, but I stay. Why do I stay? So that I can tell people I live in Gemstone Terrace. The almighty. If it were up to me … if it were up to me, I'd pack a suitcase, sock that asshole Dunboro in his pretty little face, drive away and never look back. Nothing's what I wanted. And you know the worst part? I don't even know what it is that I wanted. Or want. I just know that everything feels wrong and," he shook his head and lifted his hands from his lap, "every day I wake up reminded of that."

It was the kind of emotional flood that Tulsey had only seen twice before — once when Monica found out she was pregnant and once when her mother learned that her best friend had breast cancer. Tulsey had had a few floods herself, and though she knew what it was like to have hot emotion bubble from her lips, she was nobody's expert in giving advice. She had stood by, dumbfounded, offering little more than the presence of a warm body when Julie had made the decision to get an abortion. Having a warm body, she supposed, was better than solitude.

"I don't— " Tulsey stopped to clear her throat and say a silent prayer that she would find the right words. "I think— "

"It's like nobody even really knows who I am," Warren interrupted her. "How did I get so far away from who I am? How do you go about fixing your whole life?"

"In bits," Tulsey said.

Warren considered this for a moment. "Everything's a mess. A fucking mess," he whimpered the words like a young child complaining about a skinned knee. "Nothing is what I thought it would be. Even into my twenties I had some idea of what I was working toward. I wanted a good job. I wanted a house. I got those things, but it's not like I thought it would be." He put his head in his hands again, and his shoulders shook, though this time with a little less fury than before. After a few moments, he looked over at Tulsey and asked, "Would you believe me if I told you that, if I could, I'd give up everything I have just for the chance to start over? For the chance to not feel like I'm a prisoner to the goals I developed when I was seventeen?"

"Yes," she said, "I'd believe you."

She fiddled with her fingers and looked around the parking lot. She couldn't help but think how she was, in some ways, Warren's opposite. She had no plan when she was seventeen. She had nothing but complacency until she was twenty-nine and her mother was diagnosed. It took a family crisis to spur her to action. She had to suddenly face the fact that she wasn't going to be able to live in the farmhand house on her parents' property forever. Sooner or later, life was going to change with or without her permission. So she left Ronnie's Deli, left Monica, left her parents, left all of Lichten behind so she could go make something of herself. She had stayed complacent for so long, and now she was frustrated with her lack of personal and professional progress. She was still putting checks in numerical order and collecting a paycheck with digits so dismal she sometimes had to fight back tears. This was not what she was expecting, but here was a man who had done everything right — college, graduate school, the whole bit — and he was the one sobbing on the steps. Perhaps all roads eventually led to the same place. She had no answers for him, nor any words of wisdom. She had to hope that her silence would be enough.

Warren took a deep breath and looked up at the sky. He cleared his throat and rubbed his hands through his hair, then glanced around the parking lot.

She waited for him to stand up before she moved. When he stood, he offered her a hand and they made their way together toward the car. The muscles in her face ached – she supposed from the pinch of concern. She supposed, too, that Warren had a similar feeling in his face, along with the dull ache behind the eyes that came subsequent to a good, strong cry.

In the distance, Tulsey could hear students, fresh out of class, clanging through double doors and pitter-pattering down steps. What was once a silent slab of cement, decorated only with empty cars and the grating glow of energy-saving parking lot lights, was shifting. She was grateful for the window of quiet privacy that the universe had allowed for her friend.

EIGHT

The first snow of the season had all melted by late December, leaving Valiant with the standard winter dressing of soggy, brown, patchy grass, naked trees and tired bushes. Everyone seemed to be schlepping through the days just as they always did, leaving their driveways as the sun was coming up and returning hours after dark had settled in. Julie had grown tired of looking around the neighborhood and seeing quiet, empty houses waiting along the streets for their owners to return. She yearned to see life breathed into the streets — children riding bicycles, parents carrying in groceries or yelling at the dog to stop digging up the grass. Thinking back, Julie thought that when she and Mark first moved in there had been more people around. It used to be a destination. Now it was a pit stop.

Most of the residences in Gemstone Terrace, though empty for the majority of waking hours, had been thoughtfully decorated with lights, wreaths, and garland held up by big red velvet bows. All month, as Julie had been driving in and out of the neighborhood to run errands or go to interpreting jobs, she marveled over the decorations, not because of how beautiful they were, but because everyone around her seemed to have the energy to put up Christmas decorations. The true miracle of the holiday season, she thought, was the fact that people could somehow carve out enough time between getting home from work and making dinner to attack the front lawn with tangled strings of lights, plastic figurines, and a staple gun.

Tulsey had managed to wrap one bush in Julie's front yard with multi-colored lights that were left over after she had helped Julie and the kids put up and decorate the tree. They had gotten it up just in time for Julie's family to arrive.

Sylvia, Julie's mother, was a gray-haired, proper woman who had worn only turtlenecks during the winter for as long as Julie could remember. Sylvia tried to be helpful, and she was, with such things as laundry, cleaning, and cooking. Years ago, Julie had realized that staving off fights with her mother took an enormous amount of energy and that, all things considered, life was easier not having her around. But it was Christmas, and along with Sylvia came her father Conrad — the wisest man she knew — and her younger brother Andrew, who was witty and engaging. Conrad was a brilliant, quiet man who was generally agreeable.

They had all arrived from Ohio the night before, and Julie was grateful they planned to be around for the whole week. It would kill the boredom and isolation she feared with Tulsey away for the holiday. Tulsey had come over to meet them and have a cup of coffee, but she had gone back to her apartment to pack so she could head home. She would be gone for a week and a half.

Julie chatted politely with her mother while her brother chased Matthew and Lila around the house, trying to keep them from getting hurt or knocking something over. Conrad had taken up his usual position at the kitchen table, hunched over a newspaper and mug of lukewarm coffee.

It didn't take long for Julie's mother to start.

"I can help a little bit. Maybe I'll plan a weekend trip up here in the spring. But you know, Julie, your family can only help so much. We all have our own busy lives and our own commitments," Sylvia said, seemingly out of nowhere. They had been talking about local Christmas lights displays, and Julie had said she had not yet taken the kids to see the one in Valiant. She hadn't asked for help, but she decided that her exhaustion and exasperation had to be visible on her face. Julie could hear what was coming next before her mother even split her lips.

"And you knew what you were getting into when you married Mark," Sylvia said. "He makes a good living. You hardly have to work at all, and you have a nanny. I never had a nanny."

There it was. Amidst the fresh Christmas tree, the tightly wrapped packages, and the plate of steaming cinnamon buns on the coffee table was the cruel attempt to sever any sense of solidarity Sylvia may have had with her daughter. Julie knew that saying such things had to make her mother feel better, which was why she said them. Nonetheless, the "suck it up and be a woman" approach was not what Julie needed. Not what she needed at all. Her mother seemed to have no pure sympathy — she gave no hint that she understood that her daughter was simply stuck in a terrible situation for which no one could have appropriately planned. Oddly enough, her mother spoke as though Mark was the one always in the right while Julie was the one not pulling her own weight.

"Tulsey's not really my nanny," Julie said. "She just sort of helps sometimes."

"Great, so she's a lazy nanny at that."

"Mom, you know that's not what I just said."

It had to be her mother's own sense of powerlessness to help that drove her to lay the sole responsibility for the marriage squarely on Julie's shoulders. All Julie wanted was recognition that her situation was difficult and would be for anyone, including the strongest of wives in the strongest of marriages. Giving that reassurance was clearly beyond her mother's capability.

Julie thought about explaining to her mom that often, in her own mind, she compared marrying Mark to going to the dentist. She had a sense it was going to hurt, but she couldn't anticipate how badly. When she went to the dentist, she expected that just when she thought she couldn't stand the scraping and pinching and poking and drooling anymore, the dentist would roll his stool back, tell her he was done, and hand her a new pink toothbrush. In the long run, Julie was always happy she had gone to the dentist, but it was anything but pleasant while she was there. She wanted to explain all of this to her mother, but she didn't yet know how her own story would end. She wasn't sure her husband was going to finish before it got too painful. She was still waiting for her pink toothbrush. And she was beginning to realize that some people sat in the dentist's chair and did not get up again until he had pulled all of their teeth and all they had left was a bloody mouth, full of stitches.

"I'm going to go upstairs and see if Mark has emailed," Julie said. She wanted to get out of the situation before she told her mother what a miserable person she thought she was being.

Once she stepped into the office, she felt her stomach tighten. She was afraid that Mark had not emailed her, and that she would then have to either lie to her mother or be truthful and face further instruction about being independent and not requiring so much from Mark emotionally. She flipped her laptop open and logged into her email account. She saw an email from him with "Merry Christmas to My Love" in the subject line. She clicked open the message and read it through with a mounting sense of relief mixed with disappointment that this four paragraph electronic message would be the whole of her Christmas experience with her husband.

Julie,

As I write this, I am imagining you trying to figure out how to wrap the baby doll we bought Lila at the big Mercer's closeout sale in the early spring. I still can't believe we went to buy a stove and came back with two bags full of toys for the kids and no stove! Figures!

Things here are the same. The food tastes a little better since we've gotten a new kitchen manager. He insists on putting at least one spice in everything he cooks. Sometimes he only has access to one spice, and he puts it on everything he makes and it all starts to taste the same. I'm getting together with some of the other guys a couple nights a week now to play cards – Texas Hold 'Em, mostly. And I've started playing chess – can you believe it? Never thought I had the smarts for it. I used to make fun of people who played, but I learned it's a great way to keep your mind off things.

The chaplain's holding a service for the Christian guys at seven on Christmas Eve. I will hopefully be done with the stuff I have to do around here in time to go. Christmas day we are having a ham dinner. If it's as good as the turkey was on Thanksgiving, I'll be a happy man.

You'll have to write and tell me all about how it is with your parents and your brother and how the kids liked what Santa brought them. My mother sent a box that I hope is there by now. I left you a little something in a shoe

box on the top shelf of my side of the closet. Hope you like
it.

     Merry Christmas. Love to the kids.

—Mark

This was the best he could do? She wondered. Talk about Lila's baby doll, Texas Hold 'Em, and the ham dinner he's expecting? For the love of God, this was not a Sunday stroll together. This was one of only a handful of messages she'd gotten from him that month. This was her Christmas note that spoke of nothing but the mundane. Did he not know how hard she was working every day to keep things together so he would have a home and family to come back to? Did he not sense that she had been through a trauma? That she had had to make a family decision by herself because he was not there to be a part of that decision?

She wanted an apology, God damn it. She wanted him to feel bad for letting her down, for leaving her – again – and just expecting that everything would be taken care of. Some months ago, after the abortion, Julie had stopped thinking about what was rational. Nothing about the situation seemed rational, so why should her feelings have to be? It was true that she had not told him how she was feeling. It was also true that she had not told him about the abortion. But it was his duty to know, or at least be able to tell that something was wrong. It was his responsibility to take care of his wife the way she took care of him.

Julie did not type a response. She closed the laptop and walked slowly to the closet. She pulled down a pile of Mark's sweaters that were on top of the shoebox, then pulled the box from the shelf and lifted off the lid. Inside, nestled in with some pictures and letters Julie had written Mark on his first tour of duty, was a navy blue velvet box. She ran her thumb over the top, feeling its soft bristles beneath her skin. She flipped it open to find a white gold ring with five modest diamonds set across the top. They twinkled at her like little trapped stars. She had always worn a plain gold wedding band, as Mark had not had enough money to buy her an engagement ring. As the years passed and they did have enough money, they had talked about wanting to get her a diamond, but it was an errand that got pushed to the back burner.

She thought about the night Mark had asked her to marry him. He had not gotten down on one knee and, because of that, it had taken Julie by total surprise. They were sitting in a small Italian restaurant in the small Ohio town where they had met, having a tremendous laugh over a most bizarre couple they had been introduced to at a friend's holiday party. Mark leaned over the table, tenderly took her hand and said in a near whisper, "Marry me." It wasn't a question. It was a command. Though he was spellbound, he was still a military man. Julie had felt nothing in her heart but "yes." It wasn't the typical engagement story like the ones her friends excitedly told. It was better.

This diamond ring felt like it wasn't hers. It felt like she was trying it on in the jewelry store. Mark had not warmed up the box with his hand before he gave it to her. She knew that if she put it on, she would have to tell people he gave it to her. She would have to talk about him — perhaps even answer questions about him she was not the least bit prepared to address. Her thoughts about him had become like a sore, covered only by a thin layer of scab that could be ripped off at the slightest tug of a thought of him.

Julie didn't take the ring out of the box. Instead, she closed it, placed it back in the shoebox and covered it again with Mark's sweaters. As long as the ring remained in the closet, dealing with her marriage would be safely paused, waiting for her to address it when she once again had the strength to open the closet door and pull on the light string.

***

Though Tulsey had offered to take the train and had even lined up a ride to the train station with Warren, her father had insisted he come pick her up for her holiday trip back home to Lichten. Her father had brushed off the four-hour one-way drive, insisting that he needed to get out of the house. He had asked her mom's best friend to come to the house for the day, so he didn't have to worry about leaving his wife alone on the farm.

Tulsey smoked a cigarette at the top of her stairs and tried calling Monica for the third time that morning. Monica either didn't pick up or wasn't around. Tulsey was desperate to see her best friend. Monica had told Tulsey when she left that she felt betrayed. Tulsey told her she'd eventually understand. Monica told Tulsey to stop being patronizing. That was pretty much that. Monica had not indicated any desire to visit Tulsey. Tulsey missed Monica, but not enough to go back into the thick of things in Lichten and deal with the life she had left behind. But now it was Christmas, and there was no getting around it, so Tulsey thought she'd try to make nice in advance.

As she waited for her dad to arrive, she could hardly believe her own nervousness. She'd never been scared of either of parents. But things hadn't gone exactly as she'd thought they would in Valiant. At first, she didn't call as often as she intended to. She was frequently too exhausted from work, or in a bad mood. It seemed like every time she planned to call, Julie had asked her at the last minute if she would take the kids. Eventually, when Tulsey did get into a routine of calling them every Sunday evening, she got the feeling that both her mom and dad were deliberately making the conversations short. She wasn't sure if it was because they were angry with her, disappointed in her, or simply because they wanted to cut the cord and help her better transition to her new life. This trip being her first home since she had moved to Valiant, she was about to find out which it was.

When she saw his brown truck pull onto Nacre Court, she quickly put out her cigarette in the coffee can she used as an ashtray and went inside to get her bags. Her father, dressed in jeans, boots, and large quilted vest over a flannel shirt, met her halfway down the stairs and took her duffle bag, limping with it to the back of the truck where he hoisted it up and over.

"Damn, it's good to see you," she said, hugging him. She struggled to get her short arms around his potbelly.

"How you doin' sweetheart?" He smiled widely, revealing his nicotine-stained teeth.

"Okay," she said. "I'm okay." She caught herself as she nodded exaggeratedly.

They got into the truck, and Tulsey stuffed her backpack down at her feet. Before they drove up Nacre Court, Tulsey looked at the Curran's house and saw that Julie and the kids were waving from the front bay window. Tulsey waved back and put on her seatbelt.

"So tell me how life is," her dad said.

"It's not bad. Not bad at all. I'm starting to like the people a little more, especially Julie. She's very good to me. And Warren, the guy across the street, is a friend of mine now."

"He your boyfriend?"

"Nah," Tulsey said, picking at her short fingernails.

"And work, how's work?"

"Oh, Lord, don't get me started," she said. "They give me all the stupid people work, you know, putting cleared checks in numerical order before they're stored, that type of shit."

"They don't know the intelligence they're wastin'."

"I don't exactly have great work experience, Dad."

"You worked at Ronnie's cuz you liked it. Nothing wrong with that," he said.

"Guess not, but it doesn't get you anywhere in the jobs around here."

Her father got onto the highway, and the truck struggled into third, then fourth gear. He pulled out a pack of cigarettes and offered her one. She gratefully accepted and pulled out a lighter, first attending to his cigarette and then her own. They both ashed out their respective windows, almost exactly at the same interval.

Her dad was right. She did stay at the deli for so long because she loved it, especially the customers. She thought briefly about one customer she had had there, Mrs. Shackelford, for whom she had developed a real affection. Mrs. Shackelford came to Ronnie's every morning and had the same thing: two eggs over medium and a cup of coffee, black. Every time she took her first bite, a drop of runny egg yolk would land on her chin. After a while, Tulsey picked up on this and would always show up at her table, under the guise of checking on how the food was, to deliver an extra napkin. Even when Ronnie had to raise the prices three years ago, Mrs. Shackelford went on still paying the old charge of $2.75 for her breakfast. Tulsey had said something to her about it once, but then had let her be, quietly adding an additional two quarters to the cash so she could continue to enjoy what could only be described as Mrs. Shackelford's passive resistance. And Ronnie always had some witty one-liner to drop that would make Tulsey laugh out loud. Almost everyone in

Lichten had come into Ronnie's at some point or another, and working there was her way of keeping tabs on the whole town.

Tulsey threw her cigarette butt out the window. She put her head back on the seat and watched as the houses and buildings became farther and farther apart. She hadn't realized how tired she was. Actually, it was more like a deep weariness that weighed on her bones. Only now, in the comfort of her father's presence and surrounded by the smell and feel of his old pick-up, could she really let go. She closed her eyes and slipped into sleep.

When she opened her eyes again, she was surprised to see that she had slept through almost the whole ride. They were driving down Smith Road toward number 365, the number she had been writing on forms and letters for thirty years. She was thinking of apologizing to her father for falling asleep for so long, but instead she sat up with a start.

"What the hell is that?" she asked, pointing to the front yard.

"Tulse," her father started. He looked at her but did not finish his thought. The car crunched over the gravel driveway.

Tulsey could see everything, right down to the turtle shell glasses the real estate agent in the picture was wearing, as if the "For Sale" sign on her front lawn were in high definition.

"Have … have you had any offers yet?" This could not be happening.

"Not just yet, but we've got a couple coming over tomorrow afternoon to take a look at it," her father said.

"Christmas Eve?" she scoffed. "You're having someone come look at our house on Christmas Eve?"

"These days, you've gotta be accommodatin'. Not a lot of buyers out there," he said. "Besides, the house never did look better than it does now."

It looked like her father had finally gotten around to painting the window trim. The dead azalea on the side of the house had been dug out and replaced with a holly bush, which was covered in red berries. Pine needle garland was draped around the front of the door, punctuated with a gold and white bow at the top. Twinkling white lights peppered the front bushes, and the old white lamp post had been wrapped in thick red velvet ribbon, making it look like a giant candy cane.

Inside, the tree was in the front window, just as it always was, and its scent mingled with that of cinnamon apple cider. A ball of mistletoe hung in the doorway between the foyer and the living room, and bundles of holly were fastened to the end of the stair railing. Presents were under the tree, resting on the red quilted tree skirt that Tulsey's grandmother had made some thirty years before.

"Did mom do all this?" Tulsey asked, wanting some indication of how her mother was doing without asking directly.

"We did it together," he said, picking up her suitcase and carrying it to the stairs.

"I thought I'd stay in the farmhand house," Tulsey said. "That's my room."

"Nah," he said. "We've cleaned it all up and we don't want to have to straighten it again before the couple comes tomorrow. We planned on having you upstairs in the guest room."

He limped up the stairs with her bag. When he got to the top, he turned and looked down at her over the banister.

"I'll put this in the guest room, and then I'm going to grab a nap before dinner." The floorboards in the old farmhouse squeaked as he made his way on down the hall.

Tulsey took her jacket and hung it over the rocking chair in the corner of the family room. She rubbed her icy face to bring the blood flow back. Her mom, who had been outside, came in through the back door and made her way through the kitchen into the family room. She hesitated for a moment when she saw Tulsey. In the seconds that her mother stood still looking at her, Tulsey imagined all the reasons her mother had to hate her. She had every right to be angry. When the going had gotten tough, Tulsey had jumped ship. Sure, she moved so she could have a chance at a better life, so she could work on a career, consider going to college and give her future family a better life than this beat up town could offer. But maybe she could have waited until her parents didn't need her so much.

"Hi, Mom," Tulsey mustered.

Her mother stepped closer and put her arms around her daughter, giving her a tight squeeze.

"Come," her mother said, motioning to the kitchen. "Have something to drink."

As her mother walked down the hall, Tulsey could see that everything about her looked the same except her longer hair, which was loosely piled in an off-center ponytail instead of her usual bun. With steady hands, her mother took a teacup and saucer down from the cabinet and poured it nearly to the brim with hot water from the kettle. As Tulsey took a seat on the cushioned chair of the kitchen table, her mother pulled out a drawer and retrieved a tea bag. She dipped it carefully in and out of the cup and then set it softly on the placemat in front of Tulsey. She filled another cup, dipped in a tea bag and set it at her place at the table.

"The house looks gorgeous. Dad said you did most of it."

"It does look nice, doesn't it?" her mother said.

Tulsey took a spoonful of sugar from the jar on the table and dribbled it into her tea. She stared as the grains melted. Her mother leaned forward and rested her elbows on the table. She held her cup up near her lips and looked at Tulsey.

"How are you feeling, Mom?"

"I'm fine. Pretty good, actually."

"I'm — " Tulsey looked at her mother's silver eyes. "I'm sorry that I left. So suddenly, I mean. I've been meaning to apologize, but I thought it would be best if I did it in person." That wasn't entirely true. She had thought about it, somewhere in the back of her mind, but she had been so overwhelmed with what was going on with Warren and Julie and with work and taking care of the kids that she hadn't so much as begun formulating what she really wanted to say. That was why she was surprised she had come out with an apology so suddenly. She reconsidered her approach. "I've just been so wrapped up in myself — in making things work in Valiant — that I've dropped the ball on being a good daughter." That was God's honest truth.

"You had to do what you had to do, Tulse," her mother said. "I understand that. And letting go is part of a parent's job. I've realized that over the last few months. I just didn't realize you were so unhappy here."

"I wasn't unhappy here, Mom. I just couldn't shake the feeling that I was missing something. I felt like I had to make a move right then — like if I didn't get out, I'd end up married, have a couple of kids, take over the farm and live my whole life here."

"My grandfather built this place from the ground up. It's part of who we are. But things change, and your father and I have to adapt."

"I never thought you guys would sell so soon after I moved. I guess I just figured you'd give me the chance to come back if it didn't work out in Valiant."

"We weren't going to wait for things not to work out for you, Tulse. That wouldn't have been the right thing for us or for you."

Was this the same woman who sat across the table from her eight months ago and told her she didn't know what she'd be giving up? Who had told her that she was obviously too naïve to know what she had going for her in Lichten?

"You sound so resigned," Tulsey said.

"We have to move on. This place is not our future any more. We need a smaller home, somewhere we can have a little help with things."

"So you're going to do that by moving to an old folks' home? That's what you need? To eat JELL-O and chicken soup all day and sit around watching game shows? This place — you need this place. It keeps you active. It keeps you healthy."

Her mother stood up, walked to the counter, and placed her cup in the sink.

"This isn't all about you, Tulsey," she said, her back to her daughter. "We know what we need. You just let us live our lives and we'll let you live yours."

She rinsed out her cup and placed it on the drying rack. Tulsey watched, stunned at her mother's firmness. Tulsey was used to getting the last word.

"Dinner'll be at 7:30," her mother said before she disappeared into the hallway.

There was no turning back. Nothing was going to be as it had been. The one daring thing Tulsey had done in her life had come back to smack her in the face. Her parents had decided they'd teach her a lesson by way of selling off the land her family had occupied for more than a hundred years.

She took her teacup, a fragile porcelain affair decorated with blue and pink flowers, and hurled it at the kitchen wall. She delighted in the sound of it smashing into a thousand pieces. She looked at the broken pile on the floor and waited for the sound of one of her parents' voices, calling from upstairs to make sure she was all right. The call never came.

The doorbell rang half an hour early the next day. The couple who had arrived with the real estate agent was scarcely in their thirties. She was tall and elegant, with loose brown curls that she had gathered in a ponytail with a blue silk scarf. She wore a long black jacket that was tied at the waist and had pastel flowers embroidered at the wrists. Walking around the farmhouse, she looked like a slender queen lounging in her royal robe. He, too, had brown hair, and a finely chiseled face with unnaturally tan skin for December. He wore a dark wool sweater, cargo pants, and a red scarf tucked neatly beneath the collar of his leather bomber jacket.

Tulsey was thrilled to see such an urban couple — this house surely was not what they'd be looking for. The wallpaper in the kitchen had thin yellow stripes with a red rooster border. The family room walls were dark, and the carpeting, once long and fuzzy, was now rough and matted down. This couple wanted a new house. The farmhouse was lived in, somewhat musty, and though charming, it was anything but flashy. She sat in the family room and began to flip absently through a year-old issue of *Time*. Her parents shuffled awkwardly around the house, trying to stay out of the way.

"I really like the staircase, but this little back room over here is odd – dark and not really good for anything," Tulsey heard the woman say. "I certainly wouldn't want that to be a guest room. Too small. Maybe an office or a storage room."

The "odd" room had been Tulsey's grandmother's bedroom. It was intended to be a study, but since her grandmother could no longer walk up stairs when she moved in with them, her father had set up a twin bed and a portable rack for hanging clothes. The room was still decorated with needlepoint pieces her grandmother had done, some hanging on the walls and two more gracing the fronts of pillows that lay on the twin bed.

When the three visitors made their way around to the kitchen, their heels clicking across the hardwood in the dining room and echoing throughout the house, Tulsey was surprised to hear both the man and the woman say they liked the kitchen. It must have been the view of the farm from out the back window that made it appealing.

"How many acres?" the man asked.

"Two hundred and seventeen," the agent answered. "Plus all of the livestock, two fully functioning barns, a farmhand house, and several pieces of equipment. If you like the place, we can, of course, go over all of the elements and their estimated individual values. Let's go take a look at the grounds."

Tulsey figured she might be less humiliated if the bank had just come to take the property and sold off all their belongings at a public auction.

They were gone for more than half an hour, poking around in the private crevices of the farm. Tulsey read and reread a profile of a soldier who had lost both his left arm and left leg in combat. She briefly wondered if, at this stage, she'd be willing to trade lives with the guy. She heard them come back in. When they walked into the family room, Tulsey got a good look at the couple, and she realized they looked like they had just driven over from Valiant. It was clear that they had no business running a farm. The woman looked as if she'd never so much as had a blister on her hand. Tulsey smiled politely and looked back down at the magazine.

The couple inspected the window frames, the built-in book shelves and the brick around the fireplace.

"Oh, look, John," the woman said after she opened the coat closet in the foyer. "They have height lines marked on the inside of the door. We need to do this for Alexis." She looked at Tulsey. "Were these for you?"

Tulsey couldn't believe that this woman — this total stranger — had the balls to open up one of the closets with her sitting right there. And the tone she used, that tone she had heard so much of when people spoke to her in Valiant. It was as if the woman thought Tulsey was thirteen. Tulsey did not respond, but stared at her to give indication of how much of an infraction this whole situation was. This house needed to belong to another family. It needed to go to a family who understood rural living and who respected farming as a profession rather than thought of it as a quaint weekend activity.

After they scrutinized the bedrooms and bathrooms upstairs, the couple left and the realtor promised to let Tulsey's parents know if they decided to put in an offer.

Her mother asked for her help in preparing for the next day's Christmas dinner. Tulsey put down the ragged magazine and followed her into the kitchen. She hoped her mother did not still want to talk about the situation. To her relief, she was all business. She cleaned the turkey and got it situated in the pan. She set a pot to boil so she could make the mashed potatoes.

"You wanna grate the cheese? I need about two cups for the top of the corn pudding," her mother said.

Though Tulsey was always assigned to the menial task of cheese grating when it came to holiday dinners, she did not protest as she usually did. Instead, she dutifully ran the block of cheddar back and forth over the sharp nubs of the grater. She wondered where she'd be next year for Christmas, and whether her cheese-grating services would be required. From now on, they might just eat at some tired buffet for which the retirement community would surely overcharge. The potatoes would be instant, the gravy thin and runny, and the turkey drier than a desert sidewalk. Tulsey winced as she thought about having to choke down such a meal for every Christmas from now on, every Christmas that they were still around.

Though Tulsey's eyes were heavy with exhaustion from the emotions of the previous day, she was the first to awaken on Christmas morning. It was barely light outside when she lifted her head, unable to fall back asleep after rolling over at least a dozen times. She put on her slippers and terry cloth robe and crept down the drafty hallway toward the stairs. She was careful not to make the floorboards creak. Her mom had left the tree lights on all night, and their warm glow against the dark blue ending of night made waking up slow and calm. As she stood looking over the presents beneath the tree, she had time to be alone with her memories of the house. She had time to remember when what was wrapped under the tree was all she needed to be happy.

She went to the kitchen and poured herself a cup of coffee from yesterday's leftover pot. She warmed it in the microwave and took the steaming cup with her to the back door. There, she traded her slippers for her father's work boots and trudged through the back yard on her way to the barn. She pulled the rusty iron lock across and freed one door, slowly pulling it open. She sat down on the cold floor, her back against a hay bale and listened to the occasional snorts of the pigs and cows.

She could tell most of the animals apart, but none of them had ever been named. It was her father's policy. The one animal they had named was Billie, the small female goat that had never produced a drop of milk. Billie was so pathetically small when she was full grown that it seemed especially cruel to sell her for meat, since she wouldn't produce enough to even feed one family for dinner. Plus, she was cute. She had really long, floppy ears and abnormally large eyes. They had made a family decision to have Billie as the one farm animal mainstay.

Tulsey got up and walked over to Billie's tiny stall. She had her own space, and Tulsey could see now that her father had been in the day before to muck the stall and change her water. Though farming had always been a business for her mother and father, they did have a special tenderness for this one, pathetic little animal. Or perhaps they had tenderness for all of their animals, and they only stopped trying to suppress it this one time. Tulsey stepped over the small wooden sides and into the pen, where Billie was curled on her hay, staring at Tulsey with her huge brown eyes. When Tulsey sat down next to her, Billie reached out and nibbled on her robe, almost causing her to spill her coffee.

"No, Billie," Tulsey said.

It was cold, so she moved up close to the goat and began stoking her soft ears. She could feel the grit building up under her fingernails as she rubbed the animal's back. She breathed deep to take in the earthy, salty smell of the goat's coat.

"I don't know what to do, Billie," Tulsey said out loud, too deep in thought to be embarrassed that she was speaking to a goat. She couldn't stand the thought of her parents losing the farm. It was home like nowhere else could ever be. At the same time, the idea of walking away from pursuing her own dream after less than a year made her stomach churn. She could see Warren's face in her mind, close to hers, his expression vulnerable, capable, and kind all at the same time. She could see every curve of his face. She would die to touch it.

She imagined what Julie would say if she quit and left her to find someone new to help keep the household together. She could see Julie's brow pinch and thought about how she would answer questions about why she was leaving. Was it too much work? Was the apartment too small? Did she want to be paid a small stipend? None of those reasons. None of those reasons.

Tulsey could see Robin Marks snapping her employee file for Tulsey shut and muttering something about where to leave the office key before unceremoniously closing the conference door behind her. Robin wouldn't care enough to ask why.

Tulsey shivered, both at the cold and at the unfolding reality that she was straddling two worlds, and that one would have to ultimately win out. She desperately wanted her parents to stick it out on the farm until she either made a go of her life or decided it would be better after all to move back to Lichten. But her parents had to watch out for themselves. Their needs were changing. They had already given her so much.

"They deserve to have control over their own lives," Tulsey said. Billie's ears flopped when she looked up. The goat once again reached her nose over and clenched her dull teeth firmly on the sleeve of Tulsey's robe.

Tulsey took the last sip of her coffee, which had gone cold, and headed back to the house. She found her mother awake and in the kitchen, working on getting the turkey into the oven. The old black boom box played a CD of Christmas carols from the corner of the kitchen, and her mother had set out a coffee cake. The fact that there was no family close by didn't stop her mom from going all out on Christmas. She invited all five of the families that live on Smith Road, and a couple of families she and her dad had known since they were kids. Today would be the last Christmas dinner with all of the usuals attending.

"Everyone will be here at one," Mrs. Winslow told Tulsey when she saw her walk in. She didn't ask what Tulsey had been doing outside in the cold in just her bathrobe.

"Okay," Tulsey said. She sat on one of the stools at the kitchen counter and watched as her mother rolled out dough for the pies, the undersides of her arms jiggling with each movement of the rolling pin. Her mother was a very physically strong woman because of all the heavy lifting she did around the farm. Tulsey had always thought of her arms as firm for a woman her age. Had they been jiggling for long?

"Want me to do that?" Tulsey asked.

"I'm fine, but thanks, sweetheart. Why don't you go into the foyer and get all the Christmas cards. I saved them in the basket on the table so you could open them."

Tulsey refilled her coffee and shuffled over to get the cards. She sat down at the table and opened them dutifully, one by one. Gene and Louise Tisdale had a picture of them on the Great Wall of China. Mark and Evan Lansci were going into third and fifth grade, respectively and were both still enjoying soccer. Marilee Stevenson was divorced — finally — and had taken up going on cruises with her single girlfriends. She was "keeping positive."

Tulsey read each of the notes out loud, laughing with her mother about how every person had their own way of making their life sound better than it probably was.

"I'm still waiting for someone to write 'Still just getting by' as their holiday message," Tulsey said. Her mother snorted.

Tulsey took a large card sealed in a green envelope and slid her forefinger under the back flap to open it. She pulled out a card with a picture on it of one child pulling another on a sled around a large pine tree. It was heavily doused in aurora borealis glitter, meant to signify snow, which fell in tiny sprinkles onto Tulsey's lap. Inside it read "May You Enjoy the Small Pleasures of the Season." It was signed by her mother's favorite cousin, Len. There was a letter folded in quarters, and Tulsey opened it and read it slowly, top to bottom, so her mother would be sure to catch every word. She finished it and recited the signature line, "Bopp, love and miss you."

Her mother stopped moving the rolling pin. She stood up, wiped her hands of the flour that was on them, and placed them on her hips. She looked up at Tulsey.

"What?" Tulsey said.

"Nothing," her mother said.

But she looked confused. Lost, almost, in her own kitchen. She did not go back to rolling dough, but instead walked over to the window and looked out at the silo.

"Are you okay, Mom?" Tulsey asked after a minute.

"I'm fine," her mother said, convincingly. "It's just that for the life of me, I can't remember who calls me Bopp."

Tulsey's blood ran cold. She sat on the stool and stared at the refrigerator. With shaking hands, she carefully placed the letter on the counter.

"Cousin Len calls you Bopp, Mom," Tulsey spat out, angrily, as if she were reminding a five-year-old that it was not acceptable to eat ice cream for dinner.

Her mother tilted her head back, exaggeratedly.

"Of course," she said. "Duh, Cousin Len, of course." She laughed and tapped her forehead with the heel of her hand.

Tulsey did not wait to see what was going to happen next. She felt short of breath. She needed some fresh air. She thrust open the coat closet and grabbed her father's parka, throwing it over her shoulders.

She took off running down Smith Road, wiping tears, feeling the cold of them smeared across her face. She hadn't grabbed gloves, and her bare fingers were starting to sting. Like so many times in high school after she had gotten in an argument with one of her parents, she instinctively cut left through the Thorstons' yard and headed for Monica's, her father's boots on her feet coming untied and kicking up old muddy snow as she blew on her fingers to keep them warm. She would have relished a night when all that had caused her to rush out of the house was a ridiculous disagreement with her mom or dad about a curfew. In the distance, she could see guests arriving at the Carvers' place, covered in their dress coats and wielding holiday casseroles wrapped in tin foil. She didn't look down at her robe. She didn't care if everyone in Lichten saw her running through the neighborhood in her robe.

When she got to Monica's front door, she banged on it hard, as if the pounding were able to drown out the noise of her thoughts. Monica would know what to say. Monica would light up a cigarette and go into some long diatribe about how this whole situation wasn't fair and how Tulsey did the right thing moving and how her mom just had a brain fart and how she would be fine, just fine.

No one answered the door. She hit the thick wood again and again with her reddened hand. When there was still no answer, she ran around to the window and tried to peer in past the sheer drapes. No sign of anyone around.

"Monica — it's me. I'm sorry. Can you — would you answer the door? Are you there? Please? I need to talk to you." Her voice echoed through the icy air. She felt like she would tear apart if Monica didn't open the door.

Tulsey sat down on the front steps and put her head in her hands. This couldn't be the way things were going to happen in her family. Today her mom couldn't remember Cousin Len's nickname for her, tomorrow she would forget where she was going while on her way to the bathroom, and the next day she wouldn't remember Tulsey's name. How had her father been living with this for so long? How long had it been this bad? Why hadn't he called her to tell her? Did he wait until she came home so she could see for herself and be rotted by guilt?

She sat on Monica's front steps for almost half an hour. Had one of Monica's neighbors been around to see Tulsey's hysterical knocking and then her inordinately long stay on the stairs, they surely would have come out to see that she was all right. But all the neighbors were gone, probably all away spending time with their families. It was Christmas, after all. So Tulsey sat alone with no one to hear her knocking and no one to see her tears.

When she saw the Nelson's old green Cadillac making its way along Smith Road to her house for the dinner party, she leaned over, retied her dad's boots, tightened the belt of her robe and began the slow walk home.

The next morning, Tulsey pressed hard as she folded her clothes and packed them in her suitcase. She had lied and told her father that Julie's family had to leave early and so she needed her back that night to watch the kids. She had emptied her savings account to buy a train ticket back to Valiant on such short notice. She zipped her suitcase and called downstairs to her dad.

"You ready already?" he said.

"Yup."

It took her father several tries for the truck to get going in the cold. Once they were on their way to the train station, Tulsey lit a cigarette and stared out the window.

"Yesterday was the first time something like that happened," her father said.

Here we go, she thought.

"I mean, that was the biggest thing she's ever forgotten. I don't want you to think that I wouldn't tell you if I thought she was going downhill real fast. Prob'ly just the stress of the day."

"What if it wasn't just the stress," Tulsey said, looking over at him.

"If it wasn't it wasn't. Not much we can do about it. I'll let you know how things go. You know, I'll call."

"What am I going to do, Dad? Say you call me next week and tell me she's horrible. Then what? I can't make it better." She felt a strange rage toward him. She wanted to grab him and scream in his face that her mother was dying and ask why he didn't fucking do something.

"You should know how she's doing. You should want to know."

Tulsey rubbed her lips together hard and looked back out the window.

"What if I don't? What if I don't want to hear about it or see it or know anything about it?" She was yelling. "I'm too fucking young to take care of my mother. Christ." The words must have stung him, she knew, but she could not keep them from coming.

He held onto the steering wheel and carefully watched the road ahead. He cleared his throat and navigated. When he finally spoke, his voice was even and stern.

"This ain't all about you, Tulsey." He spit out her name. "This ain't all about you."

Tulsey shook her head and sucked on another cigarette until they got to the train station. After so many months of being away from home, her father had finally come out with how he really felt. She got out of the car, grabbed her suitcase and slammed the car door shut without saying a word.

NINE

The meeting room in the Gemstone Terrace Community Clubhouse buzzed with fluorescent lights and smelled like a lemon. It was still light outside at almost 6:00. Winter was starting to noticeably wane. Warren slipped past a brunette woman and her children and took a seat near the middle of the crowd. Tulsey had told him of the impending vote about whether Mr. Johnson would get to keep his magnolia trees. Very much to his own surprise, Warren had found the motivation to get off the couch and show up at the Gemstone Terrace Homeowners Association meeting. When Warren saw how many people were there, he decided that this must be a bigger showdown than he had anticipated. He surmised that every neighbor he had ever seen was in attendance, along with several dozen he had never laid eyes on. Apparently, the feud between Rick Dunboro and Louis Johnson had become the talk of the neighborhood. Warren wasn't sure what, if anything, his presence would achieve. He wasn't planning on speaking up, but he did hope that Mr. Johnson saw him in the crowd.

Warren looked around the room, inspecting his neighbors in such a light for the first time. He could see in their pale eyes that many of them were feigning interest in their conversations because they were too tired to end the interaction gracefully. He saw Brenda Dunboro arranging napkins and cups at the refreshment table. When she finished, she sat in the corner of the room, next to her daughter. The girl did not acknowledge her mother when she sat, but instead went on eagerly tapping away at a text message on her phone. Brenda crossed her legs and her arms, and sat, slightly hunched over, staring at a nearby bulletin board. Her face was beautifully done up and she wore a pink cardigan with rhinestone buttons. But she did not have the vigor — either in expression or posture — that Warren had come to expect from her. He didn't make a habit of judging body language, but Brenda usually carried a force of undaunted confidence that was so strong it was impossible not to notice. Tonight, she was a different woman.

The door opened forcefully, and Julie and her kids poured in, with Tulsey not far behind. Tulsey saw him in the crowd, and they all came over to sit next to him.

"Rick has to be the biggest dick I've ever met in my life," were the first words out of Tulsey's mouth. She tried to whisper them into Warren's ear, but, as usual, she had trouble keeping her volume down. Matthew turned and looked at her, but thankfully stopped short of asking what the word "dick" meant.

"Is Mr. Johnson coming?" Warren said.

Before Tulsey could answer, Mr. Johnson struggled through the door. It took him several tries to get through the door successfully with his walker. Each time he misaimed, its metal legs dinged the doorframe. A man sitting nearby came to help, but Mr. Johnson waved him off and eventually made it through on his own. He wore a dark green blazer, a white oxford shirt, and brown corduroy pants that were fastened with a belt around his thin waist. His face carried a look of fearlessness. Warren had not seen too much of Mr. Johnson over the years. It was usually hard to get a good look at him because he was always sitting beneath the shadow cast by the awning over his porch. Under the meeting room lights, he looked like he might just start swinging his walker around, clanging his snoopy neighbors in the head.

"Why are all these fucking people here?" Tulsey tried whispering to Warren again. "Are they afraid Mr. Johnson's going to croak in his house or something? Rot for three weeks before being found by some distant relative? I bet they're afraid their property values will go down because rumors will start flying around about the stench of death emanating from Gemstone Terrace."

"You're all fired up, aren't you?" Warren asked, looking at her. Her white face was red in the cheeks, and she fiddled incessantly with her straight black hair, first putting it in a ponytail, then taking it out, then putting it back again. She was adorable. Pretty, even.

"Maybe they all just want to see Rick get a kick to the teeth," Warren said.

"We should be so lucky," Tulsey said, settling into her seat and taking Lila onto her lap.

Mr. Johnson came to the end of their row and sat next to Julie.

"We've got a lot of work to get done tonight, so let's go ahead and start. This meeting is called to order." Rick's voice came through just a bit too loud over the microphone.

The chatter stopped almost immediately and those still standing sat. Warren suddenly became aware of a sort energy coming from where he sat. He and his neighbors had formed a line in the second row that began with Mr. Johnson and ended with him. He wondered if Tulsey or Julie or Mr. Johnson sensed the aura, too. Warren looked down the line and then looked forward to Rick. He felt the way he imagined the students to feel in *The Breakfast Club* when they all stared at Principal Richard Vernon. The neighbors were a unified force, there because they believed in doing the right thing. Fuck the rest of the room.

"Don't worry, everything will work out fine," Warren heard Julie whisper to Mr. Johnson. "People know Rick is a little nuts."

Mr. Johnson nodded and rubbed his palms together.

There were a number of items to get through before the big show. The board had to decide which musicians and vendors would be at the Community Spring Jazz Festival, whether to keep the same landscaping company that was currently taking care of the common grounds, and at what intervals they should place doggie poop bag dispensers along the footpath that no one ever used. When it was finally time for the board to discuss the future of Mr. Johnson's trees, Rick pulled out a large brown accordion file and sifted through it.

"Tonight, as many of you know, we will be taking a vote on the trees in Louis Johnson's yard," Rick said. "Before we take the vote, everyone on the board will have a chance to speak, discuss the matter, and ask questions. I would like to start off by reading aloud Section 14F of the Gemstone Terrace Homeowners Association bylaws." Rick shifted the papers in front of him and raised his voice slightly. "Each member of the Gemstone Terrace community is required to keep his or her property clean and presentable. This includes, but is not limited to, the following: keeping trash and recycling bins inside the garage or some other concealed area except on pick-up days; resurfacing driveways every three years, or when they show visible wear, whichever comes first; keeping lawn grass at a three-inch height or lower; keeping flower beds and other areas not covered in grass free of weeds and invasive plant species; trimming back bushes and shrubs if they are growing over walkways; having tree branches professionally trimmed if they are hanging near power lines." He paused for a moment for what had to be dramatic effect. "And professionally removing trees if their root systems are in any way threatening the integrity of another home, structure, or drainage system." He put the sheets of paper down on the table in front of him and looked up at the audience. "I have spoken with a public works official from the City of Valiant, and he is here to testify that the roots of the two trees in Louis Johnson's yard are, in fact, encroaching upon the drainage system at the end of Nacre Court."

With this, a man in a stiff blue suit stood up from the crowd, carrying with him a large illustration board.

"Good evening, ladies and gentlemen," the man said. He buttoned his suit jacket with one hand. "As Rick mentioned, after several site visits, I have determined that the roots from the trees in question are, in fact, threatening to damage the drainage pipe that leads from the edge of Nacre Court to the south end of the golf course pond. I would like to ask everyone to take a look up at the board so they can see a diagram of the estimated current state." The man pointed a long, boney finger. "As you can see, the roots are just shy of hitting the edge of the drainage pipe, and when they grow in further toward the metal, they will likely displace one section and push it away from the others, causing the water to seep into the soil instead of down the pipe."

"When you say 'just shy,' about how much space are we talking here?" asked the board member whose nameplate read Michael Ward.

"About a foot and a half," the man answered.

"Well, what's the likely time frame before a tree of this type – what is it? A magnolia? – extends its roots a foot and a half?" The board member, who Warren was quickly coming to appreciate, asked.

"Likely a matter of months," the public works official said.

"Well, I think if it's a matter of months, the trees should be removed now, as their growth will only accelerate over the summer months, and

I'd hate for us not to take pre-emptive action," said board member Molly Price.

"I couldn't agree more," Rick said. "Why would we wait around for Nacre Court to flood before we do something about this problem?"

"It's not a problem yet," Michael Ward said. "And if it does become a problem, will it flood all of Nacre Court?"

"It's difficult to say exactly what will flood, but the low-lying areas will be the most susceptible," the official said.

"But it appears, from the illustration, that Mr. Johnson's yard is the lowest lying area on Nacre Court," Michael Ward said, steadily, apparently unaware of his mounting heroism.

A fragile-looking red-headed woman in the audience raised her hand. Rick pointed to her, and she stood up before she spoke.

"For the record, my name is Jenna Williams, and I live on Citrine Street. I think it's invasive to make one of our neighbors change something that only stands to flood his own property."

"It has the potential to flood the whole court," Rick barked. The woman sat, and he continued. "Since my yard is closest to Mr. Johnson's, it's the most likely to sustain damage if this problem is not taken care of."

"Certainly your yard isn't any closer to Mr. Johnson's than my yard," Julie said, without standing or raising her hand.

Rick ignored the comment.

"How much rain would we have to have to actually overflow Mr. Johnson's yard and flood the whole court?" Julie asked, peering over the heads of the people seated in front of her.

"A significant amount, but it's certainly possible," the public works official said.

"Like, Hurricane Katrina rain?" Tulsey blurted out. She looked at Warren and bit her lip to keep back the pull of a smile.

There was silence, broken by another board member. "I understand the argument for preemptive action, but I think it makes sense to revisit this issue in another six months or so." Four other board members nodded in agreement.

"We've agreed to take a vote on this tonight," Rick said. "It would be a violation of the by-laws to put it off. Certainly, waiting is not the prudent thing to do, but I have to respect the board's decision. So, unless there are others who would like to comment, I make a motion for a vote."

"I second that motion," Michael Ward said.

"All in favor of requiring Louis Johnson to eliminate the trees on the west side of his property say aye," Rick said.

Three "ayes" arose. Rick looked to his left and then his right with disbelief.

"All those not in favor, say nay," Rick said.

Five "nays" resounded.

"Well," Rick said, "then this is settled. For now, anyway. Thank you, ladies and gentlemen. Meeting adjourned."

Warren focused his gaze on Rick, interested in how such a seemingly undefeatable man would handle not getting his way. Rick wore very little expression as he packed up his papers. But when he got up from behind the table to thank the Valiant city official, he paused for just a moment. Warren could swear he saw the muscles of Rick's jaws rippling as he clenched and shook the city official's hand.

Warren instinctively looked to his right to see if Tulsey had caught Rick's subtle but unmistakable distress. Tulsey turned to Warren, her dimples deepening as a warm smile broadened over her face.

***

The next night, Tulsey sat on the wooden stairs outside her apartment door, flicking the ashes from her cigarette into the coffee can. Her fingers hurt from the hours she had spent that day sanding down the sides of a small bookcase she was building. She looked at her nails – they were dirty and chipped, as usual. She took another drag and looked at the sky's deep purple behind the twisted silhouette of budding branches.

"Hey, you," Warren said. He was walking down the driveway, but Tulsey could make out little more than his white T-shirt as he walked across Nacre Court. "You feel like coming over for a bit?"

Tulsey felt a pulse of adrenaline. She told herself to stop it, to calm down. Warren had given her no sign that he was interested in being anything more than friends.

"All right," Tulsey said. "Lucky for you, I don't have plans."

"No plans on a Friday night, huh?" Warren said.

"Nope."

Tulsey put out her cigarette and closed her apartment door. They walked together across the cool grass, and, once inside, Tulsey flopped onto Warren's blue couch, trying to act casual.

"You got any beer?"

"I've got better than beer," Warren said.

"I like the sound of that," Tulsey said.

He disappeared into the kitchen for a moment and came back with a small wooden box. He sat next to her and opened the top, revealing a plastic bag of weed and a glass pipe.

"That box is falling apart — over use?" Tulsey winked. "I could make you a new one."

"It's built like shit. I made it in our shop class."

They both laughed.

Warren unzipped the bag and carefully packed the bulb of the pipe. He took a lighter from a drawer in the coffee table and held the flame over top, slowly sucking in until the leaves started to smoke. He passed it to Tulsey and she took a small hit first, then went for a deep, long drag.

"It's been a while since I've smoked weed," she said.

"Me, too," Warren said. "I got it from this guy I work with. I felt like I was a college frat boy again asking for it." He laughed.

"Good thing Shaw Marketing doesn't do routine drug testing," Tulsey said. "They should. This could seriously fuck up my ability to put checks in numerical order."

"Or it could help you manage the stress of such an important job," Warren said, smiling and puffing at the pipe.

"Want to order take-out?" Tulsey said.

"Didn't take long for you to get hungry," Warren said.

"I came hungry," she said.

Warren got up and went into the kitchen. He came back with a menu for Jason's House of Chinese and Chicken and sat close to Tulsey on the couch so they could both read it.

"Buffalo wings and vegetable lo mein," Tulsey said.

Warren called in the order. He had to repeat the address several times due to the language barrier between him and the woman on the other end of the line. It didn't help that he was having trouble pronouncing the name "Nacre Court." He kept running the two words together and the woman taking his order kept asking him to spell it. He would get out "N" and "A" and then start giggling and then Tulsey would start giggling and he'd have to start all over.

Finally, order placed, Warren hung up the phone and laid his head back on the couch. The pipe sent thin swirls of smoke up into the air, and Tulsey reached for the pipe again, not wanting to waste any.

"The very first time I smoked," Warren said, staring up at the ceiling, "I was a junior in high school. It was one of those things, you know, that we had planned out for, like, for three weeks. One of my friends scored some from his older brother, and we all agreed to sneak out and meet up at this park." He sat up and looked right at Tulsey, as if he were about to tell her an intimate secret. "So that night, I stayed downstairs in the basement, pretending I was watching movies. I waited until both my parents were totally asleep. When it got to be around 2:00 a.m., I pulled myself up through the basement well window when my friend Sam came knocking. He hung his head down into that dirty, nasty window well and tapped on the glass. I was expecting him, but I pulled back the shade and there was this head hanging upside down like a bat, and I jumped and almost screamed and ruined the whole thing.

"So anyway, we walk over to this park and meet up with two other guys and just sit there on the swings smoking a pipe. The weed wasn't very strong – you know, the pothead brother sold us the cheap shit. None of us felt it very much, I don't think. When I walked home, I was just really tired. I tried to open the basement window, but it was locked from the inside. My mom had gotten up, realized I was gone and locked it, so I would have to ring the doorbell when I got back."

Tulsey smiled.

"It was a spectacle," Warren went on. "Both my parents came to the door and I'm sure I stunk and had red eyes. They gave me a lecture about how I would ruin my life with that kind of behavior and so on."

He smiled and Tulsey stared at his dimples. She imagined feeling the curls of his hair with her fingers, tracing the loops over and over again until she had felt his whole head. She looked at his blue eyes shining beneath his glasses as he spoke and she realized it was actually painful to look at him without being able to have him. Yet here he was, she told herself, with no other girl in his life and no other girl in his house except her.

The food arrived a short while later via a very friendly teenager who said in a thick Chinese accent that his name was Bob. Warren gave Bob a nice tip and spread the food out on the coffee table in a fried, saucy buffet. They drove their plastic forks into the cardboard containers without even the mention of getting plates. Tulsey took one of Warren's dumplings, dipped it in a small container of thin, brown sauce, and brought it to her lips. It was the best dumpling she had ever had, though she had to keep reminding herself through her marijuana-hazed thoughts to chew and swallow, chew and swallow. Otherwise, the food would have just sat there in her mouth while she tasted it.

"Holy shit, this is good," Warren said, shoving a forkful of shredded beef into his mouth.

Tulsey sniggered and just kept eating, trying to count her many tangled joys, but they all just ran together. They went on eating for what seemed like a long time, but when they both put their forks down and announced they were full, there was still a considerable amount of food left. Warren started packing it up to put it in the refrigerator.

"Just leave it," Tulsey said. "We'll want it again in twenty minutes."

Warren agreed and packed another pipe. He and Tulsey smoked this one down, too, and when it was finished, he reached into the coffee table drawer, and pulled out a deck of cards.

"Wanna play?" he said, shuffling them.

"Fuck no, Warren," Tulsey said. "That sounds like a lot of work. I don't want to do anything but just sit here."

"All right," Warren said, dramatically turning his head away from her. "Have it your way." He put the cards down on the table and sat back, his right shoulder pressing against Tulsey's left arm. For the first time since she had moved to Valiant, Tulsey wasn't thinking of herself as deficient or undesirable. Instead, she thought about the richness of her straight black hair, about her smooth legs, and about her breasts tucked into her bra.

Warren leaned over, picked up a plastic fork and took a bite of shredded beef. Tulsey watched as a drop of sauce dripped onto his blue cotton shirt. She leaned over, pressed her finger on the spot and then sucked her finger clean. She looked up at Warren and moved her face close to his, slowly touching his cheek and then pressing her lips against his.

Warren held onto her lightly and kissed her for a moment before he spoke.

"Tulse —" he started.

Tulsey knew it had been a mistake. She bowed her head and listened to Warren try to sputter a kind explanation.

"It's not that I don't ... I mean, I adore you," he said. "You are wonderful — one of my closest friends — already. But this ... we ... this won't really go anywhere."

Won't? Tulsey thought. What does that mean? Her brain was fuzzy and she was having trouble reading Warren's body language. "Won't go" wasn't the same as "can't go" or "I don't want it to go" anywhere. Maybe it was just semantics. He was trying to let her down easily. She had no idea what to say.

"You are an amazing woman, Tulsey," he continued, suddenly finding words. "You've brought a lot to my life – you've brought something to the whole neighborhood. And I don't want to sound ungrateful or unappreciative, but .... " He ran his fingers through his hair.

"You're just not attracted to me," Tulsey said. She wanted to hurry the inevitable. Waiting for it was agony.

"I knew — that's just it. I knew you were going to think that, and I don't want you to because it's not true. You are very pretty and I love being around you, just not in that way."

"In the way you would be with a girlfriend," Tulsey said flatly.

"Right, yes — no!" And here he took a long breath and sat back, taking a hold of one of her hands. Her face was quivering and she was trying to get used to the dramatic shift in direction the night had taken.

"What I mean is, I don't want a girlfriend. I've had girlfriends. If I wanted one now, I'd want you."

"Why are you putting me through this?" Tulsey asked. She stood and looked around the room for her shoes. He stood, too.

"What I keep meaning to say is that," he put his head down and looked at the floor as he said it, "I'm gay, Tulsey."

Tulsey stopped. She walked back to Warren and stood before him. After a moment, he lifted his head and looked her in the eyes.

"But you've had girlfriends," she said, regretting it before she even got the whole sentence out. That meant nothing. She knew it.

"I was just going through the motions," he said. "I finally broke it off with my last girlfriend because I knew she wanted to get married, and that was something I could never give her. She deserved more than me."

"God, I'm so embarrassed." Tulsey started to pace around the room. "All these months I've been thinking about you and hoping for something that was never going to happen."

"You think you're embarrassed?" Warren said.

Tulsey bit her nails. "Sorry," she said. "That was a really selfish thing to say."

"I've never told anyone," Warren said.

"What?"

"You heard me." He sat on the couch and held his head in his hands. "Not even my family."

Tulsey didn't know what to do. She was simultaneously honored and humiliated. After a moment, she sat next to Warren and put her head on his shoulder. He reached his hand around her back and stroked her hair gently.

"I'm sorry," he whispered.

"No, no," Tulsey said. "Don't say that. Don't say that at all. There's nothing for you to be sorry about."

He turned and kissed her forehead softly. "Stay over here tonight," he said. "Stay with me, Tulse."

TEN

Brenda tried to speed up her daughter's process of getting ready for bed. She wrestled her away from her cell phone and sent her upstairs to brush her hair and teeth fifteen minutes earlier than usual. Laura's protest was quickly cut short by her mother's tone of voice, which was usually reserved for times when Laura had done something really bad.

"Mom, will Dad come and say goodnight when he gets home?" Laura asked as she got under the covers.

"Of course. He always does," Brenda said, turning on the ceiling fan.

"No he doesn't," Laura said.

"Sure he does, honey. You just don't remember because you don't wake up all the way." Brenda flicked off the light and trotted through the hallway to her own bedroom.

She sat cross-legged on the bed and opened her laptop. She logged onto www.suburbansingles.com. It was a chat room where Brenda had become known by the regulars as Baker197. The name and number had absolutely no connection to her real life, and she had been pleased with her own cleverness when she devised a screen name that would conceal her identity.

"You there, honey bun?" Strikebuddy1 typed to her.

"Of course," Brenda typed back.

"Thought you were gonna stand me up!" Strikebuddy1 wrote.

"Wouldn't happen. Just got a little tied up."

"How was ur day?"

"Lonely, but otherwise ok. Did some shopping. Read a book. Watched some TV. You?"

"Thought about quitting my job and running away with you. Logged on earlier, but you weren't on, so went for a jog."

"Boss still making you work weekends?" Brenda typed.

"Talked him out of that, but fat co-worker is still being a bitch … she told the boss I was behind. Not true at all. She's just nasty. Doesn't want me around."

"What's been your favorite job?"

"Been so long ago now, but was a computer teacher for a middle school right out of college. Loved it. No money, but fun."

"What do you think about me as a teacher?" Brenda asked.

"Sweetie, you could do anything — so good at communicating. So down to Earth and fun. Most likely really good at other things ☺."

"You're bad. I'm talking about work!" Brenda smiled as she typed. She had never actually met Strikebuddy1, though she spent hours imagining what he looked like, felt like, smelled like. He was always there. He always wanted to talk. He was interested in her. In what she wanted to do. In what she liked and didn't like. In how she felt. They teased about how they would be together in bed, even though they had never so much as shared a cup of coffee. Still, as Brenda went through her days, she thought hundreds of times about how it would feel to have him touch her face. She wanted it so badly that she hardly cared what he looked like. He could be something entirely different – entirely worse than what he described and what she imagined. It didn't matter.

"Always just thinking about you," Strikebuddy1 typed.

Brenda heard the front door being pushed open downstairs and, realizing Rick was home, wrapped up the conversation.

"Gotta run. Something's come up," she quickly typed. She logged off and closed the laptop. She placed it on her night table and walked to the bathroom where she hurriedly shoved a toothbrush without toothpaste into her mouth just before he came around the corner upstairs. She wanted to look like she had been getting ready for bed.

"You're early," she said, maneuvering the dry brush around in her mouth. It was rough, and as soon as Rick had walked by her and over to his dresser, she turned on the water and faked a spit.

"Since when is 9:30 early?" Rick asked, over his shoulder.

"Just earlier than I expected you — earlier than you've been all week," she said.

When they got in bed, she leaned over and kissed him on the cheek. She curled up beneath the covers and thought about what a hard worker her husband was. He always had been. And he was ambitious as hell, too. He worked like he had a lion breathing down his neck, and he was an excellent provider. She loved him for wanting all he wanted. In a way, it hardly mattered whether he did it for the family or just for himself. He did it, and he would keep on doing it. She could see in his eyes that he was so, so tired, but he kept on going. He couldn't stop himself. He needed the work to feel like he was somebody. It was simultaneously pathetic and reassuring. She'd never have to do without anything. He'd see to that. If she could have her empty spaces filled by a couple of harmless hours on the computer every day, there was nothing wrong with that. Surely other women had done much worse.

She closed her eyes and smiled. She had finally found a way to make things work.

***

Tulsey sucked her coffee through a thin, red mixing straw. It tasted like shit, but it was warm and it had caffeine and, well, it would do. She checked her email and when she saw, once again, that she had no messages other than those pronouncing her the winner of some international lottery she never entered, she went back to putting checks in numerical order and, as usual, to thinking about Warren.

She was still getting used to the idea that things would never be as she had hoped. The intricate affection she had built up for him over the past ten months had been ripped away rapidly, dismantled like a clapboard house in a tornado. Just as a house is no match for Mother Nature, Tulsey's feelings were no match for the truth. It seemed almost pathetic now, how much anticipation and imagination she had invested in a hopeless scenario.

She couldn't figure out why, out of all of the people he knew, she had been the one he had chosen to come out to first. Maybe it had something to do with the pot, the beer and the Chinese food. That combination would loosen up anyone. Or maybe he had invented an elaborate lie just to let her down easy. She felt her face flush at the idea. A falsified allegiance to the same sex would be far worse than outright rejection. If she knew Warren half as well as she thought she did, she knew he wouldn't do that.

She was left, then, only with the consolation that he had given as much of himself as he could. They had shared a night she would never forget. Warren trusting in Tulsey was an act of kindness, the likes of which no one had ever shown her, besides Julie. It was strange to think of sharing the secret of sexuality and of an abortion as acts of kindness. Perhaps they were acts of desperation. Maybe Tulsey was just in the right place at the right time and won the honor by default.

Her thumb got sore sifting through checks, so she reached into her desk drawer and retrieved her rubber thimble. She slipped it on and continued, check by agonizing check. The longer she filed checks, the more likely she became to experience the strange sensation she had come to consider a brain burp. After hours of sifting, sorting and stacking, she would sometimes lose her place and then forget altogether which stack she was working on. It would sometimes take her twenty minutes or more of backtracking and double-checking for her to figure out where she had been and where she needed to once again pick up.

The phone rang. She answered. It was for Trish Shaw. She took a message. Trish was sitting less than thirty feet away in her office. Tulsey typed the message in an email to Trish, and, very much to her surprise, Trish came out of her office to speak directly with her.

Trish wore a gray suit, tailored perfectly for her thin frame, and black peep-toe heels that had to have been four inches high, although when she walked, she appeared as agile and as comfortable as if she were wearing sneakers. Her hair had been recently highlighted, and she seemed to have a more comfortable way about her when she approached. Tulsey temporarily entertained the idea that perhaps Trish had come to respect her enough to be more casual with her as a co-worker. She approached the front desk looking like she wanted to gossip about some juicy rumor – perhaps of an office affair two colleagues were carrying on.

"Hi, Tulsey," she said, in a long, drawn out way, just the way the popular girls did when they saw Tulsey at the roller skating rink in the seventh grade. "How are you today?"

She had never once asked Tulsey how she was. Something was definitely going on.

"I've been meaning to talk to you about something – a new strategy, if you will, that I've spoken about with our accountants." She leaned forward on the front desk, showing her shiny raspberry nails.

"Oh?"

"These cancelled checks that you've been working on – that you've been doing an excellent job with, by the way – most of them, I believe, are more than seven years old, correct?"

"Yes," Tulsey said.

"Well, you know how we like to be very thorough here."

Tulsey gave an obligatory nod.

"We cross all our T's and dot all of our I's."

Tulsey nodded again.

"Even though we like to keep excellent records, we've decided that we just don't have the space for all of the old checks. And since the accountant assures me that we would not need them if we were audited, I'm going to have to ask you to get rid of them."

"Get rid of them?" Tulsey said. She felt like her stomach had just dropped out of her and splattered on the floor like afterbirth. "What?"

"We'll need to shred them, of course." Here she gave a little laugh, throwing back her head as though she were almost too charmed with herself to stand it. "We can't very well just throw them in the dumpster."

Tulsey felt a cold tingling run the length of her spine and spread out to her should blades.

"And by 'we' you mean 'me.'"

"What?" Trish asked.

"You mean me. I'll be the one to shred them."

"I can have one of the marketing associates help you, if you're having trouble doing it on your own."

Tulsey stood up and ran her tongue along the inside of her cheek as she glared at Patricia Shaw, the illustrious owner of Shaw Marketing, whom she had once thought she might like to trade lives with.

"You're asking me to put the last ten months of my work in a shredder?"

"There's one in the conference room, and if that one has any problems, feel free to buy a new one. We'll reimburse you for it."

"Oh, I see," Tulsey said, pacing back and forth. "How nice. You'll let me actually pick out the shredder that I use to destroy ten months of my work?" She was starting to raise her voice, and, though she stopped for momentary reconsideration, she ultimately decided to hell with it. Who gave a shit anymore? It was all starting to fall apart anyway. Or maybe it was never together. Her mother was dying and she had left her. She had left her for the sad existence of a wannabe suburbanite. A wannabe suburbanite whose love interest was gay, whose job was the farce to end all farces, and whose home life now consisted of a broken military wife, her two young children, and the soulless community they inhabited.

A look of concern came over Trish's face, as if she were finally starting to comprehend.

"This is the first time in ten months that you've ever asked me how I was," Tulsey said. "Do you know that? Are you even aware of that, Trish?"

"Well, no, I ... I ... " Trish stammered and backed away ever so slightly from where Tulsey continued to pace.

"And the one day you do ask me, you tell me that everything I've done for you has been for nothing."

"Oh, no, Tulsey," Trish said in a syrupy voice. "I would never say that it's been for nothing. Of course it hasn't."

"Oh, don't patronize me, for Chrissakes," Tulsey said.

Trish's eyes widened.

Tulsey leaned over and took hold of her purse. She grabbed her coffee mug, which was still half-full, and the picture of Billie the goat she had stuck next to her computer.

"I quit," she said.

Trish rolled her eyes.

Tulsey forced her way past her from behind the receptionist's desk. On the way, she caught her hip on the side of one of the boxes of checks, and it slipped off the table, spilling a flurry of yellow rectangles. The last thing Tulsey saw in the office of Shaw Marketing on the seventh floor of Somerset Tower, Suite 714, was the sight of the checks coming to a snowy rest on the floor next to Trish Shaw's designer four-inch heels.

On her way out of the building, she stepped into the ladies' room next to the first floor lobby and pulled off her pantyhose. She rolled them into a tight ball and pitched them into the wastebasket, then put her shoes back on.

Waiting for the bus that late morning in the spring sunshine was far more pleasant than usual. She was suddenly struck by the fact that she had nothing for which she needed to hurry home. It was still five hours before she was expected to take over for Julie with the kids. She sat pleasantly on the bus stop bench, and for what she guessed was only the second time, she really saw her surroundings. There was a quaint children's clothing store on the block, and she thought it odd that she had never before noticed the pillars that flanked its front door. They were made of stacked three-dimensional shapes, and each was a different pastel color. There was a park across the street and up about a block and half – had that always been there? Of course. It must have been. It had lush green grass, some sort of fountain in the middle, and was edged with blooming daffodils. Tulsey watched as a young woman corralled her toddler son across an intersection while she shuttled a blanket-covered baby in a stroller.

"Do you know when the forty-five usually comes?" a stout woman with a slight mustache asked over Tulsey's shoulder.

"I imagine it will be around eventually. I don't usually ride at this time of day." Tulsey took a deep breath and felt the sun on her face.

The woman let out a combination of a sigh and a grunt and marched over to the corner. She hailed a cab, and Tulsey watched as she stuffed her briefcase and her duffle bag into the back seat.

A few moments later, the forty-five bus squealed up to the stop, and Tulsey sat pleasantly in the second row. She held her purse on her lap and watched as the bus lumbered past the cab holding the mustached woman. It was stopped behind a delivery truck. On the ride out of the city, Tulsey leaned her head back on the seat and closed her eyes, napping on and off in the heat of the sun that was beaming through the window. When the bus finally rolled to a stop on Emerald Drive, Tulsey got off and decided she wasn't quite ready to go back to her apartment. Navajo Joe's would be a perfect place to waste an hour or two. She could read the paper and stave off the inevitable conversation with herself about her choice to quit in such spectacular fashion. Before she berated herself for the consequences of her actions — not just quitting, but getting herself into the whole mess of Valiant in the first place — she needed to have an intimate celebration.

The wind chimes sang when Tulsey opened the door at Navajo Joe's. She swaggered to the counter and ordered a Lakota Latte with whipped cream and three shots of caramel at forty-nine cents a shot. The whole affair was more than four dollars, but it was damn good. Like creamy heaven. Every previous trip to Navajo Joe's, Tulsey had ordered a small brewed coffee, only half caffeinated, and had done it up with Splenda and skim milk. It was the cheapest thing on the menu, it was low-fat, and had less caffeine. All of those restrictions were completely inappropriate for a celebration. She chose a large leather chair beneath a bull's skull and horns mounted on the wall. She licked the whipped cream off the top of the coffee and savored the taste of the salty-sweet caramel flavor on the back of her tongue. Out of the corner of her eye, she caught a glimpse of Brenda Dunboro. She turned her head to look and made eye contact with Brenda, who quickly looked away.

That bitch did *not* just pretend not to see me, Tulsey thought. Fueled by the power of her own will and her own sense of right and wrong, both of which she had already exercised thoroughly that day, Tulsey decided to get up and go over to speak with Brenda. If nothing else, this woman would learn that you did not make eye contact with a neighbor at the local coffee shop and pretend you didn't see them. She would know that Tulsey would not stand for the cold disrespect that Brenda executed with everyone when it suited even her most fleeting whim. She stood up, caramel Lakota Latte in hand, and marched over to Brenda.

"Hello, Brenda" Tulsey said loudly. She sat in the open seat next to her. "How are you?"

Brenda snapped her laptop shut and gave a smile. "Tulsey," she said. "Nice to see you."

"You didn't see me," Tulsey said, shortly. "I saw you."

Brenda laughed uncomfortably and leaned away from her, looking out the window as if she were fascinated by the minivans with no apparent destination, rolling around in the parking lot like a line of carpenter ants.

"Did I interrupt something?"

"Oh," Brenda stuttered, "no. Not at all. I was just reading."

"Really? What were you reading?" Continuing this conversation and watching Brenda squirm because she had been called out on her rudeness was nothing short of delicious.

"The newspaper," Brenda responded. "Online," she added, unnecessarily.

"Do you frequent Navajo Joe's?"

"Not really," Brenda answered.

There was a kind of silent stand-off for a while, which Tulsey won when Brenda finally could cope with it no longer and filled the silence with a question.

"What are you doing here at this hour?" Brenda asked. "Don't you work as a secretary or something downtown?"

"I quit my job today," Tulsey said triumphantly.

"Why?" Brenda asked.

"Because my boss – my former boss – decided it would be best if I just shredded all of the checks I have spent the last ten months putting into numerical order."

"Why would she ask you to do that?" Brenda seemed to be growing increasingly interested.

"Because she's fucking incompetent and didn't ask her accountant what she needed to keep and what she could get rid of."

"And where was this?"

"Shaw Marketing."

"So she paid you to do all that unnecessary work?"

"She paid me to sit there, answer the phone, and kiss her ass," Tulsey said. "I think the directive to organize the checks was just a whim." Tulsey shook her head. "I really don't think she had any idea how many hours of my life I put into that."

"So you just quit?"

"So I just quit," Tulsey repeated.

"What do you do now?"

"Haven't thought about it yet, but what I do know is that I won't be anyone's bitch."

Brenda sat stiff and dazed-like in her chair, one hand on each armrest, the laptop perched on her thighs. To Tulsey's astonishment, the glisten of tears was in the corner of Brenda's eyes as she sat gazing at the milk bar.

Suddenly, Brenda drew in a rapid breath and threw her hands to her mouth to muffle a beastly sob. She stood up and walked briskly to the bathroom, one hand still over her mouth. She closed and locked the door behind her. Tulsey followed a few moments later and knocked.

"Brenda, are you all right?" she asked. There was no answer. "I'll just be waiting out here if you decide you need to talk," she said through the door.

Ten minutes later, Tulsey had bought herself a newspaper and was sitting on the floor outside the door. She had to wave off several women who had come to use the restroom. She told them her friend was sick, it would be a while, and they'd be better off using the men's room. It was single-stall, just like the women's anyway.

Tulsey leaned into the door. "Was it something I said?"

The door slowly cracked open and Tulsey took the invitation to enter. Brenda was sitting on the toilet seat, holding her mascara-streaked face in her hands. Her nose and eyes were red and she was wringing her hands.

"Do you want to talk about it?"

"No. Yes. I don't know," Brenda said. "I don't even really know what's wrong. I have no idea why I'm such a mess. This is so embarrassing. I swear nothing like this has ever happened to me before."

"This is your first time crying?" Tulsey asked, trying to elicit a smile.

"Don't be such a smart ass. You know what I mean. And don't give me your pity, either. The last thing I need is your pity." She cried heartily for a moment, and when she caught her breath again, she continued. "I just ... I just wish that one time in my life I could do what you just did."

"Do what?" Tulsey asked. "Quit? It takes a real champion to quit."

"No," Brenda said. "I mean to get out of something that's not right. Even if you're scared."

Tulsey considered this for a moment. "My mother told me once that change happens when you're less afraid of the unknown than you are of the known. I guess that's what happened today. I was petrified of sitting at that stupid desk for even just one more day."

Brenda nodded.

"So, I've still got another hour or so until I have to take care of the kids. Why don't we get out of this decidedly unclean bathroom and head to my place for dinner?"

Brenda went to the sink and ran cold water over a paper towel. She wiped her eyes away and blew her nose.

"We can take my car," she said.

Tulsey dug into her freezer and pulled out two plastic containers of beef stew. She heated one at a time in the microwave and gave Brenda a beer. They sat – Tulsey on the bed and Brenda in the desk chair – for quite some time in relative silence, greedily sopping up beef stew with fresh sourdough bread that Tulsey had purchased the day before.

"This is delicious," Brenda said. "I don't remember the last time I had beef stew."

"A better day in a bowl," Tulsey said. "That's what I've always called my mother's recipe."

"I don't think I really knew Rick as well as I thought I did when we got married," Brenda said.

"What makes you think that?" Tulsey asked.

"It all used to work so well. Rick was never working like this – he's always worked hard, but this is every night, all weekend. He said last year he wanted to be able to buy a bigger house, but he hasn't been looking for places to move. I think," she paused here, as if to let the pain of thinking the words pass before she said them, "I think he might just want to spend as much time as possible out of the house."

"Have you told him you want him to be home more?"

"Many times. Maybe not in the right way. He gets angry when I question him about the hours he's working. It just never seems to be enough money for him. We have so much. Way more than either of our parents ever had, but to him, it's not good enough."

Brenda looked around on Tulsey's desk, and her eyes landed on a photo album. She pulled it from the shelf.

"Mind if I look?"

"Sure," Tulsey shrugged, thinking the request a bit odd, but not wanting to deny Brenda anything that might make her feel better or at least offer her a bit of distraction.

Brenda went through the pages slowly, poring over pictures of Tulsey's childhood. There were many of Tulsey and Monica together. In one, they were on the farm riding horses, in another they were dressed up for Halloween, and in still another they wore high school graduation gowns. There was a picture of Tulsey as a teenager holding Billie the goat when she was a baby. There was a photo of Tulsey sitting with her parents in the grass at a Fourth of July picnic.

"These your parents?"

"Yes."

"Your mother is gorgeous," Brenda said.

"Thank you," Tulsey said.

Brenda put down the album and walked around the apartment, seemingly soaking in every detail of the art on the walls, the magazines piled on the dresser, the flowers in the vase, the bumper stickers on the closet door. Brenda came to the mother-of-pearl vanity in the corner and leaned down to look closely at it. She ran her fingers over the top.

"Where did you get this? It's exquisite. It must have cost a fortune."

"Nah. Picked it up at a garage sale for forty bucks. It's probably a big piece of junk, but it makes me think of a big pearl, and I love pearls, you know, for metaphorical reasons."

"Metaphorical reasons?"

"All pearls start out as a grain of sand."

Brenda continued inspecting the vanity, curiously feeling its brass legs.

"Oh, shit," Brenda said, suddenly noticing the time. "It's almost seven. Laura is going to be dropped off soon. I've got to go back to the house."

She put her shoes back on and grabbed her sweater from over the back of the desk chair. Tulsey held the screen door open for her. When Brenda was halfway down the wooden stairs, she turned back to look at Tulsey.

"I think the known just got scarier than the unknown."

Tulsey gave only one nod.

Brenda turned back and made her way down the street and back to the other side of Nacre Court.

ELEVEN

When Julie made it to the top of the stairs, she could see through the screen door that Tulsey was in the kitchen washing dishes. She knocked on the doorframe, and when Tulsey didn't answer, she called her name. The faucet stopped.

"Hey. What's up?" Tulsey said, opening the door. She wiped her hands with a dish rag and looked at Julie expectantly. An unannounced visit was not Julie's usual way of contacting Tulsey. She had wanted to be respectful of Tulsey's privacy, so she almost always called her before coming by. But she had gotten a phone call from Mark and she had instinctively gone to Tulsey as soon as she hung up the phone. Julie hadn't given herself time to think it through. The kids were napping and she hadn't known what else to do. Now, as she stood before Tulsey, knowing the news would affect her greatly one way or the other, she felt her forehead start to sweat.

Tulsey had a look of resignation. Julie wondered if it was because she had guessed the news in the seconds since she had knocked on the door.

"Mark's coming home," Julie said. She rolled up on the balls of her feet when she said it. With her hands in the pockets of her jeans, she suddenly became aware that she was exhibiting the body language of kindergartner who had just been caught eating paste.

Tulsey smiled. "I'm glad."

"I don't know that I am," Julie said.

"Do you want to sit down? I've got some coffee," Tulsey said.

"No, thanks," Julie said. She could feel herself growing increasingly agitated. She wanted Tulsey to say something that would straighten out the snarl of emotions she felt, but it didn't come. Tulsey stood silent, apparently just as lost for words as she was.

"I think you should tell him," Tulsey said finally. "In person it's—it'll be easier."

"Will it?" Julie asked. Her eyes started to fill with tears and Tulsey came close to embrace her.

Julie rested her chin on Tulsey's shoulder. "I want you to stay," she said.

Tulsey drew a deep breath and hugged tighter but did not respond.

***

The Japanese magnolia trees in question outside of Mr. Johnson's house had exploded, seemingly overnight, with hardy pink and white blooms. The branches of the trees remained bare, however, and the flowers stood alone with the forsythia and the daffodils against the gray landscape of the fading winter.

Tulsey walked past them on her way out for a twilight stroll. Most of the golfers were gone by this time, and she would often reserve this part of the day for an uninterrupted walk. This evening, the walk took on a special significance, as it wasn't just a way to get exercise. Rather, she needed the time to weigh her options and decide, once and for all, if it was best for her to cut her losses and return home to Lichten.

Valiant was not a place for unmarried people with no children to set up shop. She had suspected that just a few weeks in, but she had kept on keeping on, hoping that the metaphorical clouds would part and a path to something better would emerge. Instead she had gotten a front row seat to the Gemstone Terrace circus.

Tulsey headed around the backside of the golf course pond and stopped for a moment to watch as the water from the creek bubbled over into the pond, causing a frothy mix of pollutants and algae to mingle at the base of the miniature waterfall.

Patience was not her strongest virtue, but she had figured that by this time she would have made some young professional friends or been on a date with at least one heterosexual man. Certainly her entire experience as an office worker had failed. The only redeeming factor about her stint with Shaw Marketing was the fiery end to which it had come, which was growing more hilarious by the day. It was amazing, Tulsey thought, how one gained perspective only when removed entirely from the situation. To her own relief, she had only regretted quitting for about a thirty-minute period two weeks ago when, while half-heartedly looking for another administrative position online, she had come across a posting for her old job. The salary they were offering was, of course, not disclosed, but the wording made it sound as though every day on the job was sure to be an engaging, rewarding experience that would be the first step on the path to becoming the successor to Trish Shaw herself. Tulsey wondered if it was exactly the same ad she had responded to almost a year ago. If so, she could hardly blame herself. After all, it was a marketing firm; they were professional spin doctors.

The grass beneath Tulsey's feet was cool with the forming evening dew, and she took the long route around the tee of the seventeenth hole. A handful of crows, eager to get in one last meal before turning in for the night, squabbled over a discarded hotdog bun on the fairway.

Tulsey thought about the fact that Julie could put an ad online and have her replaced with someone more qualified in a matter of days. The real issue, though, was that Mark was coming home. They needed to be together as a family, to deal with all that had happened. Julie may feel like she wants me around, Tulsey thought, but I would only serve as a temporary buffer. They'd both be on their best behavior at first, especially Mark, knowing they had a constant sort of house guest in Tulsey. But eventually that would fade, true feelings would emerge, and Tulsey would find herself entrenched in a family affair that she had no business even knowing about. She had done all she could for Julie. Her presence now would only hold her back.

A breeze picked up and it got chilly as the last signs of light echoed in the sky. Tulsey buttoned up her cardigan and crossed her arms around her chest against the cold.

The young couple who had come to look at her parents' farm on Christmas Eve wound up purchasing it for much more than the list price. They had gotten into a bidding war with another young couple. Her father had called to tell her when it happened, but the gravity of it didn't seem to be settling in until just now. The farm was soon to be gone, but she did still have the chance to help take care of her mother.

Almost back to the edge of Nacre Court, she sat for a moment next to the pond to watch a frog she'd caught sight of. His papery throat pulsated in and out as he balanced masterfully on a slimy rock. He began to croak confidently, dutifully, as if he were on a mountainside singing a lullaby to the entire valley below, announcing to all that it was officially time to retire the day's work and settle in for a night full of soothing rest. Never before had Tulsey seen a creature so confident in his role, so proud to perform his duty, so utterly pleased by his domain.

Hearing her thoughts in the quiet, she knew she was not imagining her mounting feelings. She knew they would not go away with time and a positive attitude. The situation was in front of her now, no longer tangled up in amorphous thoughts. She needed to go home. Her life had its own inertia, a magnetism that, if ignored, only grew in strength.

No sooner had Tulsey let this revelation escape to her consciousness than her thoughts were interrupted by the shrill voice of Brenda Dunboro, who called to her from inside her open garage door. After briefly considering pretending she hadn't heard and high-tailing it back to her apartment, Tulsey climbed through the tall grass and back onto the pavement.

"Hi, Brenda," she forced out in a quiet tone, giving a small wave and keeping her distance so as not to make herself look available.

"Tulsey, I was wondering if maybe you'd come in for a cup of coffee," Brenda said.

"Thanks, but I've quit drinking coffee," Tulsey lied.

"A beer then," Brenda said.

Tulsey thought the skin of her forehead might actually split. She threw her head back, turned on one heel and said, "Now might be the worst possible time."

"Do you have somewhere to be?"

Tulsey considered the irony of the question. She was close enough now to see the contents of the Dunboros' freakishly neat garage. And she was close enough to see the look of agitation on Brenda's face.

"All right, one beer, then I'm going home. I'm exhausted."

As soon as she was through the door, Brenda turned to her and announced that she had something important to tell her.

"What?" Tulsey asked with what she hoped was detectable irreverence.

"Come into the kitchen and sit down."

Tulsey rolled her eyes and followed her.

"Yuengling or Blue Moon?"

"Got anything stronger?"

"Rick drinks scotch."

"Perfect," Tulsey said.

Brenda disappeared into the living room and came back with a crystal decanter. She pulled off its spherical top and poured some into a glass. Then she took the coffee pot and refilled her mug. She sat down at the kitchen table and scooted in closer to Tulsey, about to spill her secret.

"So?" Tulsey asked. She took a gulp of the scotch. Had to be a single malt — it was delicious.

"Rick is planning to cut down Mr. Johnson's magnolia trees," Brenda said. There was a slight sense of excitement in her voice, and Tulsey wasn't sure if it was because she was telling her something she shouldn't or because she found her husband's aggressiveness brag-worthy.

"He hired somebody to do it?"

"No," Brenda shook her head. "He's going to do it himself. In the middle of the night. Two weeks from tonight. He's got it all planned out. He even bought a black ski mask."

Tulsey shrieked with laughter. Brenda looked at her nervously, perhaps realizing she had just made a big mistake.

"What an idiot. That's illegal. Who does he think he is?" Tulsey lifted her glass to her mouth and let the scotch burn on her lips for a moment before taking a sip. "Unbelievable," she said, almost to herself.

"I know, I know. He'll wake everybody up. Mr. Johnson will call the police. It will be a mess. But he says he can get them down before anyone can stop him. Then there won't be any more argument about it. The best Mr. Johnson can do is plant new magnolias, and they'll be much smaller — they won't block the view." Brenda paused for a moment and then went on. "And, honestly, Tulsey, he knows so many people. He thinks he'll get away with it one way or another. He's probably right. He probably will."

"So what are you going to do about it?"

"I don't know. I wanted to get your advice. I mean, what does one do? Call the police? Rick would kill me."

"Tell Mr. Johnson," Tulsey said.

"What's he going to do about it?"

"He'll take care of it if you tell him," Tulsey said.

"What if Rick gets arrested? I mean, he could be disbarred. We could lose everything."

"Oh, for fuck's sake, Brenda, stop underestimating that man. Tell him. He'd tell you." Tulsey drained her glass, set it on the table and walked out.

Brenda was silent.

"I'm going home," Tulsey said. "Thanks for the drink."

She didn't wait for Brenda to get up to follow her, but instead marched out through the front door and back across Nacre Court. She said a silent prayer to the Universe in thanks for that ridiculous conversation. She no longer had doubts about whether leaving was the right thing to do. She would tell Julie tomorrow and she would be gone inside of a week.

TWELVE

Mr. Johnson sat on the couch and picked up the shotgun that was on the floor next to the couch. He cleaned and oiled it. The dirty canvas drawstring bag that had once apparently held the gun lay across the stone hearth. He ran a rod through the barrels of the gun over and over again while the orange glow from his Tiffany table lamp illuminated his work.

So the old man had some serious fight in him, Warren thought.

"Go to the fridge and get yourself a beer," Mr. Johnson said. "This is a kind of party after all, isn't it?"

Warren obliged, and when he came back, he sat next to Mr. Johnson and snapped open the can. Mr. Johnson clinked his glass of gin against Warren's Bud Light. The night had officially begun.

"You look like an expert with that thing," Warren said.

"I should be. I've had it for long enough."

"When's the last time you had it out?"

"Couldn't even take a guess."

There was a quiet knock at the door.

"It's unlocked," Mr. Johnson called.

Brenda and Julie both slipped in quietly. Brenda looked different somehow, Warren thought. Maybe a new hair cut? It wasn't as straight as it usually was. Her face, too, looked younger.

"Go to the fridge and get yourselves beers," he said. Julie shrugged and went to the kitchen.

"Is that entirely necessary?" Brenda said, eyeing the gun.

"Depends what you mean by 'necessary'," Mr. Johnson said.

"Well, it can't possibly be loaded," Brenda said. "That thing's so old they probably don't even make bullets for it anymore."

"This is so sad it's almost funny," Julie said, walking back in with two beers. She handed one to Brenda. "To think, this is what we suburban folks do on a Tuesday night."

"It's not almost funny, it *is* funny," Warren said.

Brenda looked at him and shrugged.

"That should about do it," Mr. Johnson said, leaning the shotgun against the hearth and reaching for his walker. "Let's head outside. Brenda, shut off the lights, would you? And I'll need my drink."

Julie grabbed the glass and walked alongside Mr. Johnson to the front door.

They sat in the dark on the front porch, with Warren having to settle for the creaky wicker ottoman because the fourth chair was missing a leg. Julie moved her chair forward and stretched out her feet, resting them on the top of the porch railing. A grimy film coated the wood floor and all the furniture, lending a salty, organic smell to the surroundings. The bullfrogs down at the pond let out thick croaks and lent a pattern of sound to the night.

The four of them chatted quietly to pass the time.

When Rick finally did come, they could only see the top of his head in the weak light from his own draped windows. It bobbed up and down with his steps, but after a few seconds the silhouette of his whole body and the chainsaw he was holding came into view. His hair was tucked under a baseball cap and he moved quickly and quietly. His feet brushed against the tall grass, causing only the faintest whisper of a disturbance. Warren looked over at Julie. She sat at attention in her chair. Brenda crossed her arms over her waist. Mr. Johnson did not move.

Rick leaned his head to the side to check for anyone who might be watching him from inside the house. The shadow of the porch obscured his audience. He set the chainsaw down and inspected the bark close to the base of the trees. He marked a line on each tree with chalk and picked the chainsaw back up. Just before he was about the pull the starter cord, Brenda's voice escaped her, weak and shaking.

"You can't cut them down, Rick," she said.

Rick walked toward the porch, coming into a pool of light shining from Warren's front door. Still holding the chainsaw, he cocked his head sideways and strained to see beneath the shadow of the overhang.

"Brenda?" He was pissed.

"It's not legal and, aside from that, it's not right."

"What the fuck are you doing out here?"

"You know what I'm doing out here."

"Go back to the house," he said. "Now."

Rick walked closer to Mr. Johnson's front stairs.

"Don't come near the porch," Warren said.

Rick stopped. "Who's up there with you, Brenda?"

She didn't answer.

"I said who the fuck is up there with you, Brenda?"

"I'm up here," Mr. Johnson said.

"Me, too," Julie followed.

"And me. You know, the next-door neighbor you've been ignoring for seven years. My name is Warren."

"Jesus," Rick said, laughing, "what is this? Some kind of neighborhood coup?"

"Something like that," Julie said.

"Now go on back to your place and we'll forget this ever happened," Mr. Johnson said.

Rick turned and walked back down toward the trees, shaking his head. He stopped cold at the sound of a shotgun being cocked. He turned around and saw Mr. Johnson step out of the shadows, his wrinkled hands steady on the metal of the gun and his walker nowhere to be seen.

"I said go back to your place," Mr. Johnson repeated.

Rick laughed. "What are you going to do, shoot me?"

"Life in prison isn't a long time for an old man," Mr. Johnson said. He lifted the gun slowly and pointed it at Rick.

Stunned, Rick stammered backwards a few steps, then turned around and disappeared into his open garage.

Julie put her arm around Brenda and walked with her back into Mr. Johnson's house.

"Take this and put it away in the coat closet, would you?" Mr. Johnson said to Warren. "And get me my walker."

Warren took the shotgun and went inside, leaving Mr. Johnson to make his way in on his own. Warren picked up the canvas bag, and before putting the gun back into it, he flipped open the chamber and saw that it was loaded. His knowledge of shotguns was limited to what he had learned in Boy Scouts, but he knew enough to know that this gun could still kill someone. He pulled the shells out, placed them in his pocket, and leaned the gun up against the wall in the closet, just behind Mr. Johnson's khaki rain jacket.

***

Tulsey leaned over a circular saw, cutting planks and trying not to sneeze at the sawdust. She felt her cell phone vibrate in her pocket. She turned the saw off, set it down and pulled her gloves off so she could answer.

"Hello?" It was Warren. She hadn't spoken to him in a couple of months. He wanted to know if she would come back to Valiant to have lunch.

"I'll pick you up from the train station," he offered.

"Warren, I don't know."

"Oh, c'mon. You won't have to see anyone else. No one will even know you're here."

She reluctantly agreed. Catching up with Warren was worth the memories she'd inevitably face at the sight of Nacre Court.

They agreed on the following Saturday, and that morning Tulsey boarded the train with butterflies. She noticed it was quite a different crop of passengers than those she had ridden with more than two years ago for her morning interview with Robin Marks at Shaw Marketing. There were parents anxiously trying to get their children into seats and elderly couples dressed in nice clothes pointing at buildings and cemeteries as they looked out the window. Before, it had been mostly people dressed in starched business attire, staring ahead or at judiciously folded newspapers.

When she arrived, she couldn't help but put her arms around Warren. She still had a slight surge of adrenaline when he hugged her. She remembered his smell as though the night she had spent with him had been mere hours before.

"How's the new job?" Warren asked once they were in his car.

"I like it. I really like it."

"Seems a perfect match for you. How did you find it?"

"My old boss Ronnie told me about it when I went back to the deli to ask for my job back. He said he'd be glad to take me back, but that his sister's husband was looking to hire a cabinetmaker. I took some of my pieces over there to show him and he agreed to train me. Pay's good. I should be able to buy a place in another year or so."

"And how's your mom?"

"She's hanging in," Tulsey nodded. Unsure of exactly what to say next, she continued with the basics. "She and dad like their new place. They seem to be making a lot of friends, and, you know, they have a bunch of different activities to do. I hear mom's getting pretty good at bocce ball."

"Never too late to pick up a new sport," Warren said. His smile was still as gorgeous as she had remembered it.

Not surprisingly, everything in Gemstone Terrace looked very much the same. She felt for a moment as though she had moved away just the previous day. It was everything it used to be, just without the promise of something new. It was an old shoe to her now. It had been worn out. She had thrown it away.

When they pulled into Warren's driveway and rolled to a stop, Tulsey reached for the door handle and pushed the door open. She stepped out onto the fresh, black pavement and lifted her head to Mr. Johnson's yard across Nacre Court. There were still dandelions in the grass and two shutters were still missing, while a third was askew. Grass grew irreverently from the cracks in his sidewalk.

And there, in the early afternoon sunshine, she saw the familiar tulip-like pink and white blooms blazing from bare branches, announcing in silent triumph the arrival of spring.

Tulsey blinked and looked again. "Mr. Johnson's trees – they're still there," she stammered.

Warren looked at her, his blue eyes showing warmth she had never before seen. His lips parted into a wide smile and he nodded, still looking at her in what she recognized now as admiration.

"I thought for sure Rick would've found some way to get rid of them by now."

"Nope," Warren said. "That night was the last we heard from Rick about those trees."

She turned back to look once again. "Huh," she said. "I'll be God damned." She reached into the car and took hold of her purse, slinging it over one shoulder before she closed the door. "I'll be God damned," she said again. And with that, she turned back to Warren and, together, they walked inside.

About the Author

Brooke Kenny is a fiction writer and the book reviewer for The Gazette Newspapers in suburban Maryland.

Her fiction and non-fiction have appeared in numerous publications, including The Washington Post. She earned a master's degree in creative writing from The Johns Hopkins University in 2008.

She lives with her husband in Maryland.

This is her first novel.

www.ingramcontent.com/pod-product-compliance
Lightning Source LLC
Chambersburg PA
CBHW071219260626
47162CB00004B/1359